Acclaim for Donald Proffit's *Scapegoat*

"Donald Proffit's *Scapegoat* is one of those rare historical novels that doesn't just recreate the past—it interrogates it.... It's a grim and lyrical work that lands uncomfortably close to our present moment, and that's precisely what makes it so compelling."

—*Manhattan Book Review*

"*Scapegoat* by Donald Proffit is a vivid, haunting, and masterfully structured historical novel that delves deep into the psychology of persecution, social conformity, and forbidden love."

—*The Historical Fiction Company*

Also by Donald Proffit

Hardship, Alaska: A Memoir

The Object of His Affection

SCAPEGOAT

by

Donald Proffit

SYNTHETIC
PROPHETIC

Library of Congress Control Number: 2025906044

SYNTHETIC PROPHETIC ⇌
Kingston, New York, USA
www.syntheticprophetic.com

ISBN: 979-8-9921999-8-7

Printed in the United States.

But the scapegoat, the one upon which the burden of guilt is placed, shall remain alive. It will stand before the Lord, its body unblemished but heavy with the unspoken wrongs of the congregation, and then it shall be cast out into the wilderness—a living atonement, banished to bear the weight of what others cannot.

—Leviticus 16:8-10

Preface

The summit of happiness is reached when a person is ready to be what he is.— Erasmus (1466–1536)

Erasmus' words reflect a tragically unattainable ideal for many in the 16th century. In a society where conformity was enforced with violence and individuality was condemned as a sin, to "be what one is" could mean risking one's life. For François van Daele and Willem de Clerck, this truth was inescapable.

This tale is deeply intertwined with my own family's past. My ancestor, Susannah North Martin, was accused, convicted, and executed as a witch on July 19, 1692, on Gallows Hill in Salem, Massachusetts. She, along with many others—both women and men—became scapegoats for a society consumed by fear and moral hysteria. Her fate prompted an exploration of how societies, seized by panic and a need for control, single out and punish those they deem outsiders. This investigation led me across the Atlantic to Flanders in the Early Modern Period and into the mechanisms of persecution across time and place, which became the foundation for this narrative.

By the 1550s, Bruges—a once-thriving city now in decline—was deeply entrenched in strict religious and social norms that governed every aspect of life. Once a jewel of the Hanseatic League and a trade center, Bruges' fortunes had dwindled as silt had long since choked its rivers, canals, and ports, cutting it off from the sea. Fear and moral rigidity took hold against this backdrop of economic hardship as leaders sought to maintain order through religious and social control.

Under the rule of the Habsburgs, whose empire stretched across much of Europe, the Catholic Church's dominance was enforced with increasing severity. While not as consolidated in Bruges as in Spain, the Inquisition cultivated an atmosphere of fear and mistrust, which often led to mass hysteria targeting those suspected as heretics.

In crafting this work, I aimed to portray the historic city of Bruges in 1558 vividly. To do so, I have occasionally added street signs and names to locations where they might not have existed or been documented. While the Marcus Gerards Map of 1562 displays street names, they were likely added over time. Where appropriate, I have included some of these later-added names to establish a better sense of place and orientation for the reader.

Meanwhile, the Reformation's advancing guard of Protestant doctrines began to overtake the region, introducing new ideas about faith and individual conscience that challenged entrenched power structures, particularly the Catholic Church, and deepened suspicion among the people. Deviations from strict religious, social, or moral norms were swiftly—and often brutally—condemned.

The term "sodomy," rooted in the Biblical story of Sodom and Gomorrah, was a broad label encompassing acts such as bestiality, masturbation, same-sex relations, and even non-procreative intercourse. While these behaviors are now understood as distinct, in that era, they were all seen as grave moral transgressions—deliberate rebellions against the natural order rather than expressions of personal identity. Often enforced inconsistently, these laws were as much about maintaining social order as they were about morality. The accusation of sodomy was a weapon wielded to eliminate rivals, settle grudges, or assert dominance. François and Willem were not just accused of a crime—they became scapegoats for a society's anxieties about change, power, and control.

At the time, the age of consent was strikingly low: twelve for girls and fourteen for boys, though this applied only within the confines of marriage. Without the sanctity of marriage, sexual acts—particularly those labeled as sodomy—were deemed sins so grave they were believed to threaten the very fabric of the community. Such offenses were punishable by death, though on rare occasions, leniency was granted to passive participants or those considered less culpable.

This novel is a fictionalized retelling of the trial, conviction, and punishment of François van Daele and Willem de Clerck in 1558—real individuals caught in the web of these harsh and unforgiving laws. Imagine two young men walking the cobblestone streets of Bruges, whispering hopes and fears to each other under the shadow of a society ready to condemn them. In many ways, ordinary lives became extraordinary in their public unraveling—victims of laws that sought to control actions and the essence of being.

Joos van den Rijm, a fictional balladeer, is presented as the composer of a ballad about François and Willem years after their trial. The novel begins in 1596, as van den Rijm performs the song in a Bruges tavern—summoning the past with his words and inviting the listener (and reader) into the tragedy of 1558. The final chapter, too, leaves us in his presence, reminding us that history is never truly silent.

Though neither van den Rijm nor his ballad existed,

his presence here reminds us that history is often preserved through song rather than records. Popular ballads shaped how people understood justice, morality, and fate, turning the past into legend. Stanzas from van den Rijm's "Ballad of the Scapegoat" appear as chapter epigraphs throughout the book.

Today, as LGBTQ+ individuals continue to be targeted as scapegoats amid political and cultural conflicts, François and Willem's story feels heartbreakingly relevant. By looking to the past, we can better understand the forces at work in the present—and perhaps find ways to resist them.

Excerpts from The Summoning of Everyman (c. 1490–1510), based on an arrangement by Peter Lukacs and Elizabethan Drama (ElizabethanDrama.org), are included to deepen the reader's understanding of the era's moral and religious framework. Paired with van den Rijm's imagined lyrics, these passages provide a lens through which to view the harsh judgments and punishments imposed upon François and Willem.

Through their story—and van den Rijm's words—we enter a world where love and desire become a death sentence, and the human spirit struggles against the weight of judgment and fear. The echoes of their trial remind us that the fight for acceptance and individuality is ongoing—and that history holds valuable lessons for the present.

The Ballad of the Scapegoat

Bruges has seen many a bastard, but none sang as sweetly as Joos van den Rijm.

The poet himself would not have denied it.

Perched on an ale-stained table in The Bear, a well-worn tavern near the Bourse, van den Rijm lifted his cup in mock reverence before strumming a low, deliberate chord on his lute. The fire cast flickering shadows along the beams, darkened by decades of smoke and whispered confessions. This place had seen many men pass through its doors; some were forgotten, and some were made legends.

A hush settled over the room as he began to play, his voice curling through the smoky air. The melody wove through the tavern, drawing in drunkards and merchants alike. Some had heard it in Antwerp or Ghent, though never from the poet's lips. Others listened warily, glancing toward the magistrate at the bar, who was already scowling into his beer.

Van den Rijm played on.

"The events of 1558 are no mystery," the magistrate finally interrupted, his voice cutting through the music with brutal clarity. "Justice was done. The city purged its filth—we all took part in cleansing it. You poets love to dress up history in finer clothes than it deserves."

As the magistrate spoke, Joos van den Rijm let his fingers drift from the strings and, with casual amusement, flipped the lute onto its back, balancing it on one knee. He spun it idly, the polished wood catching the candlelight, his grin widening as if the instrument found the interruption entertaining. When the crowd's murmurs settled, he grabbed the lute by its neck, gave it a theatrical twirl, and resumed plucking at the strings as if the magistrate's words had been nothing more than a passing breeze.

Van den Rijm grinned. "Ah, but what is history if not a song retold until it pleases the powerful?"

A chuckle rippled through the crowd.

"Besides," he continued, plucking out the next refrain, "I did not invent François and Willem's fate, good sir—only the melody." He leaned in conspiratorially, smirking. "Which I stole, naturally. A good tune is wasted on the pious."

Laughter broke out, though quieter this time.

The magistrate's expression darkened, but before he could reply, a burly cooper near the hearth chimed in, raising his mug. "I heard you were thrown out of Ghent for calling a bishop a barnyard rooster. Is that true or just another of your embellishments?"

Van den Rijm sighed theatrically. "Ah, yes. The Ghent incident. A grievous misunderstanding." He plucked at his lute, adopting a wistful expression. "I meant it as a compliment! Roosters are vigilant creatures—watchful, commanding, and prone to strutting. But alas, the bishop took offense." He grinned. "Churchmen have such delicate feathers."

The cooper roared with laughter. The magistrate did not.

Someone at the bar muttered, "Didn't he try to join the court in Antwerp? Didn't last long, though."

"Yes," another chimed in, "until he had to flee dressed as a monk—ruined his disguise by singing bawdy drinking songs before he even left the city."

Van den Rijm set a hand over his heart. "You wound me, gentlemen. I wasn't fleeing—I was merely traveling at an expedited pace."

The magistrate scowled. "That ballad of yours is nothing but sedition. Tell me, minstrel—did François and Willem even exist?"

Van den Rijm's smile flickered slightly before returning to the crowd.

"Oh, they existed," he said. "They walked these very streets, flesh and blood, before the law made ghosts of them." His fingers danced over the strings again, softer, almost reverent.

The tavern fell quiet. Even those skeptical of his tale found themselves caught in the pull of his voice.

For a moment, no one spoke. The magistrate tapped his fingers against his mug, his frown deepening. The cooper shifted in his seat. A serving girl paused mid-pour, her gaze locked onto the poet as if he had summoned ghosts into the room. A flicker of something—unease, reverence, curiosity—passed through the assembled crowd. Even the embers in the hearth seemed to glow a little brighter as if eager to listen.

Van den Rijm let the moment linger—the flicker of candlelight across expectant faces, the thick scent of ale in the air, even the magistrate, despite his frown, leaning forward ever so slightly. He lowered his voice, letting it curl like smoke into the rafters. "The year was 1558..."

And as his fingers wove the first aching chords, the world outside the tavern dimmed. The walls of The Bear melted into the past, the candlelight flickered into dawn's mist, and suddenly, it was 1558 once more—where a lone peasant, cold and weary, trudged toward the city gates, a sack of fish slung over one shoulder, fear flickering in his gut...

Through the City Gates

Through Bruges' gate, a peasant strode,
Beneath the dawn's pale silver shroud.
A sack of fish, his humble prize,
Yet fear burned bright within his eyes.
In Bruges' square, a shadow vast,
A giant slept whilst whispers passed.
The bells fell still, the air grew cold—
A tale of blood and dread foretold.

The early morning mist clung to the low fields like a ghostly veil as a lone peasant trudged toward the gates of Bruges. His coarse tunic clung to his body as the chill of the dew settled deep in his bones. His cloak resembled a patchwork quilt and hung awkwardly from his shoulders, its frayed edges betraying years of wear. Cracked, thin-soled boots made each step more laborious. He was a stranger in the city, holding a small sack of salted fish, which he hoped to trade before the grand Procession of the Holy Blood began—a sacred event where a revered relic, said to hold Christ's blood, was carried through the streets in an act of devotional pageantry. Yet, as he neared the city walls, the festive bustle that should have greeted him was eerily absent.

The streets were quiet, the dawn's first light barely touching the worn cobblestones. A few vendors were setting up their carts, and distant church bells tolled softly, but the city had yet to wake fully. As he wandered deeper into the heart of Bruges, the peasant veered to the left instead of right, ending up in a narrow alley behind the grand Market Square.

And that's when he saw it resting in an adjoining alleyway.

A monstrous, hulking figure towered over the nearby buildings, even in recline, its head nearly scraping the rooftops. The peasant's heart pounded as he squinted, trying to make sense of the thing.

"A giant."

It lay slumped on its side, limbs sprawled awkwardly across the wooden wagon on which it rested, as though it had collapsed mid-stride. The creature's enormous head and painted eyes were hidden under a hood. It appeared to be sleeping, though its slackened face was far too human for comfort. Draped in tattered robes, its massive chest rose and fell with a slight breeze, creating the eerie illusion of breath and life.

The peasant thought he could hear the faintest breath escaping its lips, a low rumble that sent terror racing through his veins. "A giant..." he whispered again, his mouth dry with fear. He took a step back, his hands trembling. "Sweet saints preserve me."

Panic gripped him. He fled. His scuffed boots slipped on slick stones as he sprinted toward the city's gates, his breath escaping in ragged, shallow bursts. At last, he reached the city's southeastern portal, Gentpoort. Once outside the city ramparts and into the open, his terror only deepened as he passed the Gallows Field—a grim clearing where justice was ruthlessly meted out. Wooden posts spiked skyward, weathered by time, their ropes swaying in the breeze. Ravens roosted higher still in the skeletal branches of nearby trees, their black feathers gleaming like polished onyx against the pale morning light. Here, hangings, floggings, and burnings awaited witches, scoundrels, sodomites, and thieves alike; their punishments—quick and dead—served as stark reminders to any who defied Bruges' laws.

Beyond the field, he scarcely noticed the shift in scenery. In his haste to leave Bruges, he missed the beauty of the countryside surrounding him: tall elms and oaks, lush with new, bright green leaves, casting soft shade over the dirt road; poppies, daisies, and violets painting the roadside in red, white, and purple bursts; young stalks of wheat and barley bent and swaying in the breeze, and the hawthorn hedgerows sparkling with delicate white blossoms and dew.

He also failed to see a lone figure approaching and subsequently collided with a journeyman, knocking the man's leather-wrapped bundle to the ground and scattering his belongings across the roadway.

The journeyman brushed off his cloak, a simple woolen garment with faint creases from travel. Beneath it, his doublet—a deep blue with rough stitching along the seams—hinted at a trade that demanded functionality over elegance. His dusty but well-mended hose matched the practical sturdiness of his leather-wrapped bundle.

"Watch yourself, friend!"

The peasant, wide-eyed and frantic, bent down to help the man collect the scattered items: small weaving tools, needles, thread, and a loom shuttle sat in the dust, along with an eating knife, cup, bowl, undergarments, and a sheaf of guild papers. Among the debris, the peasant noticed the journeyman had also brought staples: hard bread and cheese, a bit of salted and lightly dried herring for protein—preferred by travelers as it didn't require soaking to soften like the hard salted North Sea cod—and a handful of dried fruit and nuts to give him energy along the road.

"You mustn't go in there!" he gasped once the man's belongings had been hastily repacked. "There's a giant…sleeping in the square. I saw it with my own eyes—its head as big as a wagon! If it wakes, God help us all."

The journeyman studied the peasant and smiled gently. There was a note of playful caution in his voice when he asked, "A giant, you say?"

The peasant nodded fervently. "Aye! I swear it. It's sleeping now, but it won't stay that way. You'd best turn back. You don't want to be caught in Bruges when it rises."

"No, friend. I've come to find a job and cannot turn away now." He gave the peasant a reassuring nod. "Whatever you saw, I'm sure there's an explanation. The city's full of strange wonders this time of year."

The peasant stared at him in disbelief, still haunted by the vision of the sleeping giant in the square. But the journeyman, undeterred, pressed on toward the gate, his figure swallowed by the thickening mist.

The peasant stood rooted to the spot, muttering a prayer under his breath. He dared not follow him back into the city; he couldn't shake the sense that something terrible was coming for Bruges—and that the giant was only the beginning.

He watched as the fearless journeyman approached the towering Gentpoort rising before him, its sturdy stone arches a testament to the city's fortifications. He paused briefly by

Gallows Field before passing through the gate as if the whispers of lives cut short beneath Justice's cold hand had called to him, stirring something unspoken within.

With a final glance toward the swaying ropes and circling ravens, the journeyman pressed onward, the weight of the city's unyielding laws following behind him like a shadow.

Ascension Day

Beneath the Belfry's restless skies,
The spire o'erwatched Bruges' slow demise.
Matthias trod the cobbled ways,
Through gilded light and shadowed haze.
The festival's bright pageants rang,
With looming giants as they sang.
The bells cried loud, the echoes grew—
Through holy light, a shadow flew.

Despite the tales of giants he had heard throughout his life—and the frantic warning from a fleeing peasant that morning—the journeyman Matthias Engel entered the fortified town unafraid. He knew the rumors were fueled by the discovery of petrified mammoth and mastodon remains dredged up from nearby fields.

The North Sea sky hung over Bruges, shifting in shades and moods with the ever-present wind. A haze veiled the city and its network of silted canals like a ghostly presence. Behind this gauze-like scrim, the sun offered restrained hope as it teased muted blues to break through and illuminate The Belfry—a symbol of the city's grandeur and a vigilant observatory for spotting fires and other threats.

Seagulls trapped in purgatorial gusts were tossed like spectral angels suspended between heaven and earth, their cries cutting sharply against the muted hum of life below. The wind tugged at shutters and scattered debris down narrow alleyways as though testing Bruges' resolve and reminding it of its vulnerability. The journeyman was captivated by this place—hauntingly beautiful and heartbreakingly adrift—a city losing its grip on its golden age as a leading trade center.

To the journeyman, Bruges was a place of contradictions: beautiful and crumbling, proud yet steeped in desperation, clinging to its past glory as if waiting for someone—or something—to bear the burden of its loss, for someone to blame.

He wandered through the labyrinthine network of cobbled alleyways and passages, letting the scents of baking bread and sizzling meat wash over him, each aroma a warm facade. Yet he found no such warmth in the faces of Bruges' people; their expressions were worn thin by years of dwindling hopes and the briny staleness of stagnant canal water. Was there a job for him here in a city so entangled in its fading past?

In overheard conversations, a cacophony of languages turned the streets into a jabber town. Flemish, French, German, Spanish, and Portuguese mingled like the sludge in the canals, stirring his curiosity and eluding his understanding. Here, voices were half-familiar and foreign, like whispers of distant lands converging in Bruges' stony alleyways.

He passed through the main square, with its enormous belfry rising above the steeply pitched roofs of guildhalls, steepled churches, and other utilitarian structures. Most had crow-stepped gabled facades adorned with finials, small spires, and stylish patterned brickwork. The roofs were shingled with clay or slate tiles. The town was vastly different from Oudenaarde, with its simple, thatched-roof buildings, small shops, and the scent of farmland drifting through.

He first encountered only a few townspeople, most

heading toward a church for Ascension Day Mass. Later, the day would unfold with a parade honoring the city's liberation from French rule in 1227 by national heroes Jan Breydel and Pieter de Coninck. The festivities would culminate, in the afternoon, with the Procession of the Holy Blood, in which a blood-stained cloth believed to have been used by Joseph of Arimathea to wipe the dead Christ's face, would be carried through the streets in its ornately decorated vial, inspiring pop-up biblical reenactments. A traveling theater troupe would take up the rear of the procession, offering a morality play to the joy of the Bruggelingen.

Matthias joined a line of townsfolk, following a family into the towering Collegiate Church of Saint Donatian to attend Ascension Day Mass. Outside, the imposing Romanesque-Gothic structure dominated the Burg Square with its intricate stonework and lofty bell tower, casting long shadows over the bustling activity of merchants and pilgrims. Inside, the energy of the streets dissolved into serenity, the damp air heavy with incense and faintly warmed by flickering candlelight. Members of the church's council of canons—priests responsible for overseeing the liturgical and administrative functions of the church—moved purposefully through the aisles, their solemn presence underscoring the order and reverence of the sacred space.

He set his bundled belongings to the side, careful not to disrupt the quiet solemnity. Men like him had no seats; in the church, the only chairs, luxuriously upholstered and richly carved, flanked the altar and were reserved for the priest and dignitaries. The high vaulted ceilings drew his eyes upward, where stained glass windows filtered soft morning light into kaleidoscopic hues, depicting saints, biblical scenes, and the life of Saint Donatian, the city's patron.

Matthias, a weaver by trade, marveled at the tapestries adorning the hewn limestone walls. He considered the hands that created these masterpieces: fingers stained and sore from the weld, madder, and woad dyes, their skin rough with calluses, lined with fine grooves where countless threads had worn paths. He ran his hand over the coarse texture of his cloak, a sharp contrast to the fine threads of the tapestries.

Paintings of the Stations of the Cross hung in gilded frames, their solemn scenes offset by the majestic tapestries whose meticulous details offered added visual narratives for congregants distracted by uninspired homilies.

A magnificent rood loft separated the nave from the chancel, its carved figures seeming to watch over the gathered faithful. Beneath it, the clergy moved deliberately through the sacred rituals of the Mass as the organ's music floated down from above, joining with the faint chanting of psalms by unseen voices. The treasury glittered in a corner near the chancel, protecting relics, jeweled chalices, and sacred manuscripts as quiet testimony to the collegiate church's wealth. Matthias's gaze lingered briefly as he approached the altar to receive communion.

He approached the altar, carefully stepping past the ranks of burning candles, and knelt to receive the Host. The priest murmured a blessing as the wafer was placed on his tongue; its dryness grounded him momentarily in the incense-laden air before dissolving in saliva. The plain unleavened bread sufficed for the laity, while the wine was reserved for the clergy. He closed his eyes briefly, focusing on the act as the delicate flavor melted away, leaving an aftertaste of divine mystery.

One of the assisting canons broke his pious stance to follow Matthias as he returned to his place beyond the transept. The man's gaze was out of place, interrupting the quiet euphoria he was experiencing—not so much from the sacrament itself as from the overwhelming beauty and solemnity of his surroundings.

The Mass ended with the chant "Ite, missa est," and Matthias followed the slow procession of worshippers leaving the church into Burg Square. From passersby, he heard of the festivities soon to begin, with people already eager to find the best spots to view the pageantry. Woolen cloaks and tunics in muted tones mingled with the brighter fabrics of merchants and artisans among the crowd. Some wore elaborate feathered hats, while others wrapped simple scarves around their heads to guard against the late morning chill.

Matthias moved from the square onto Blinde-Ezelstraat, a wide thoroughfare that promised to lead him to Market Square. But as the street branched into narrow alleyways, he veered onto a passageway with unpredictable twists and turns, and no matter which direction he turned, he found himself lost in the unfamiliar streets, and his sense of wonder with the town soured.

Hoping to retrace his steps, he glanced about, seeking a sign, a marker—anything to orient himself—but the city offered no such kindness. For all its beauty, Bruges had very few street signs, and unless you lived here for some time, every alleyway appeared no more than a random web of crisscrossing animal trails shaped by the ebb and flow of life over generations. He paused, listening to the muffled hum of voices coming from everywhere and nowhere. "The square," he muttered, "I just need to get back to Burg Square."

He crossed over a small bridge, likely part of Steenhouwersdijk. The canal's still water sharply contrasted with his growing agitation. Soon, he found himself on an even narrower passageway, where the cobblestones felt greasy and uneven. A primal sense alerted him to another presence as if he were being shadowed.

He ducked into a small alcove he thought was an alley dominated by shadows. But it led nowhere, dead-ending into a collapsed wall. He returned to where he had entered as two figures emerged from a narrow passageway between two buildings.

"Lost, friend?" one of them asked, his voice slick with false camaraderie. The man's cloak hung heavy around his shoulders, his hands resting casually at his sides. His companion, silent and wiry, flanked Matthias, cutting off any escape.

"I mean no trouble," he said, his voice wavering as he backed away.

The taller of the two stepped closer. "Well, this must be your lucky day because trouble just found you," he said.

The larger of the two men brandished a jagged-edged knife and let out a guttural growl before lunging at Matthias, his unshaven face spasming with urgency. "Hand over your belongings!" he barked.

Before Matthias could react, the second swindler—a sinewy man with piercing eyes and drool-slicked lips—scrambled from the shadows in a blur, cutting off any chance of escape with swift, predatory movements.

Matthias attempted to reason with them, explaining he

was a journeyman with nothing of value, but the ruffians closed in. Cornered, he braced himself, clutching his bundle tightly as one man lunged for him.

"Leave him alone!" a sharp voice called out from behind. Matthias turned to see two young men rushing into the alley.

The taller of the two, a boy in a brown doublet, raised his hands placatingly. "No need for trouble, friends," he said, his voice steady. The other, a lean lad with dark hair, grabbed a loose plank from the ground and brandished it.

"We'll call the city guard!" the younger one barked. The threat—and the sight of the improvised weapon—was enough to send the ruffians retreating with muttered curses.

"Thank you," Matthias stammered, brushing dirt from his cloak. "I don't know what I would have done."

"Think nothing of it," said the taller boy, extending a hand. "I'm François, and this is Willem. You're lucky we were passing by."

The journeyman eyed both boys with curiosity. "I'm Matthias Engel, a journeyman from Oudenaarde. I owe you more than thanks."

"What brings you to Bruges? Are you here for the festival?" François asked.

"No, not for the festival, but it's a pleasant diversion. I'm looking for work. I tried Ghent, but the guilds there are restrictive, especially for newcomers like me without connections. I've been moving from village to village with no luck. I'm hoping Bruges will offer better opportunities for a journeyman.

"How about you join us?" Willem suggested with a grin. "It's safer together—and you look like you could use a good spot to see the procession."

François placed a hand on Matthias' shoulder. "It's hard to find work here, too, but our guilds are less restrictive, and depending on your skills, you might find work or apprentice with a local craftsman."

Together, they backtracked along Steenhouwersdijk and found their way to Blinde-Ezelstraat, the narrow lane leading them into Burg Square. From there, they passed through Breidelstraat and emerged onto the bustling expanse of Market Square. Matthias thought, "I was so close when I left St. Donatian earlier this morning; how could I have gotten so lost?"

In the square, people gathered, jostling for the best vantage point. Matthias was swept up in the crowd and the two companions' energy. They found a spot along the square, and Matthias marveled at the number of people crowding the bustling marketplace.

Soon came the blare of trumpets, issuing a ceremonial last that startled some and brought a reverent hush to the crowd. They played on, and came into view: long valveless natural trumpets, adorned with embroidered coats of arms—a black lion on a gold field. Behind the trumpets, draped with banners bearing the city's emblem—a red shield with a white cross—a row of wooden cornets droned beneath the fanfare.

Matthias stood transfixed, silent, and awestruck as the solemn procession wound through the heart of the town. At times, he rose onto his tiptoes, straining for a better view of the men on horseback in crusader garb, flocks of sheep and shepherds, Adam and Eve, and parading characters from numerous biblical tales. Scenes from Christ's Passion unfolded before him—Christ carrying his cross, Roman guards, and the Crucifixion. The effort made his calves burn.

The Burgermeister and town officials were wearing black robes emblazoned with a pelican feeding her blood to her young and reenacting local historical events, which meshed the civic and sacred importance of the day. The many guilds showcased their apprentices, journeymen, and masters, all joining the procession culminating in the arrival of the ornate crystal and gold reliquary safeguarding a cloth stained with the blood of Christ. The weavers' guild marched proudly, their aprons dyed deep indigo and their doublets embroidered with the guild's crest. Behind them, the bakers carried loaves on trays, their white caps bobbing in unison, while the fishmongers followed with cloaks that bore the faint aroma of the sea. The clergy had the relic and were escorted by the Noble Brotherhood of the Holy Blood, whose duty was to protect and venerate the sacred object.

A mix of reverence and foreboding nearly overwhelmed Matthias at the sight of the vessel holding the sacred relic. Its solemn beauty masked a more profound, more troubling power. He realized that in this town faith was more than belief—it was a spectacle, a craft, and a force of influence. The crowd's voices rose in the familiar strains of the Te Deum; its Gregorian melody, though recognizable, sounded subtly altered from what he knew in Oudenaarde. French and Spanish influences and evolving tastes in modal music had reshaped the traditional songs, yet the hymn's solemn intent endured.

The crowd moved around him as if driven by a shared instinct—a hive, no, a pack of wolves—a living tide of lupine hunger and human devotion. Wolves had long since vanished from Bruges' cobbled streets, their howls silenced by stone walls and advancing fields. Yet it was not nature that had driven them out; men—bounty hunters, farmers, and noblemen—had sought to tame the wild at any cost. The hunt for wolves became a dark crusade to purge the untamed from the land and their hearts. Yet, as much as the wolves had been driven away, their memory endured—a shadow cast over tales of loyalty, hunger, salvation, and peril. Those who had eradicated them, in their fervor, had taken on the very qualities they sought to destroy. The procession seemed to stir this shared memory, drawing the crowd into an ancient rhythm transcending time.

Heads turned sharply, then tilted downward, tracking the relic's glimmer as though pursuing prey. Shoulders rose, and spines arched subtly as feet shuffled closer, closing the space between bodies like a pack converging for the kill. Eyes half-closed as if intoxicated with feral lust, they moved in unison, their gestures primal and instinctive. A low murmur rippled through the throng—not words, but guttural sounds that carried reverence as if the relic were the moon calling them to howl. Cloaks flared and swished in a phantom mimicry of tails while children crouched low on their haunches to peer through the shifting forest of legs, their eyes glowing with primal curiosity.

As the clergy drew nearer, their solemn chants mingled with the Te Deum's Gregorian strains, and the crowd's energy reached a fever pitch. A keening sound rose from somewhere within—a lone voice, then a harmony of cries that crescendoed into something wild and unbidden. It was not a cheer but a sound older than language, older than the faith that now bound them together. Matthias caught his breath, a shiver coursing through him. He sensed an untamed presence, not in physical form but in spirit—an unseen energy that flowed through the crowd, tethering them to something ancient, far beyond the gilded relic they revered.

With practiced precision, Matthias raised his right hand to his forehead, his movements habitual yet reverent, and traced from his forehead downward to the center of his chest, then to his left shoulder, and finally to his right, completing the prayerful gesture. His hand lingered briefly at his side, grounding him in the act. He closed his eyes in contemplation, but his thoughts lingered on the crowd's collective cry—a sound that hinted at an untamed wilderness hidden behind Bruges' orderly facade. A wilderness that the city had fortified against since its inception, but wilderness had not vanished; it had only changed form.

He caught fragments of the verses—"Sanctus, Sanctus, Sanctus, Dóminus Deus Sábaoth"—and felt the solemnity of their praise rise above the sway of the crowd, their devotion uniting them in the ancient liturgy. Yet it was the final words, faint but unmistakable as the procession turned a corner—"In te, Dómine, sperávi: nonconfúndar in ætérnum"—that lingered in Matthias's thoughts. "O Lord, in thee have I trusted, let me never be shamed." The plea struck a chord deep within him, a quiet echo of his unspoken hopes.

The fading chant dissolved as it moved farther into the town, replaced by a rising, thunderous rumble that Matthias recognized as wagon wheels. The contrapuntal interplay of wood on cobblestone created a polyrhythmic beat that underscored the groaning creaks of the wagon's timber frame and the weight of its enigmatic cargo. The sound bounced off buildings along the narrow alleys and twisting passageways, making its source impossible to trace.

Above the rumble, Matthias could distinguish a new sound—a dense clacking, like skeletal bones rattling together but heavier, somehow out of place in the familiar din. The noise grew louder, vibrating through the ground and rattling nearby windows. A massive shadow crept across buildings, and an alley opened onto the square, heralding the wagon's arrival.

As it rolled into view, the source of the sounds became clear: the heavy, groaning hubs of the wheels, creaks from the stage's weight, and that of the giant puppets suspended on top. The first thing Matthias saw was how the figures' upper body shifted slightly with each turn as if straining against the ropes and pulleys restraining them. The faces of the onlookers were in complete shock at the sight of the untamed behemoths before them. The rhythmic clip-clop of horses' hooves and the jingle of harness bells added another layer as the enormous structure entered the square, drawing townsfolk toward the spectacle of the morality play that awaited them. At that moment, Matthias fathomed what the peasant he encountered outside the town's gates had stumbled upon earlier that day. He must have seen the wagon parked in some obscure square before the day's celebrations and mistook one of the sleeping puppets as an actual giant.

Matthias marveled at the grand theatrical wagon for its artistry, mechanics, and craftsmanship, towering over the cobblestone streets. It was an imposing structure evoking awe and reverence among the townspeople as it rolled into the square, its intricate details a tribute to the story about to be told.

Matthias quickly studied the structure, beginning with its base, which was constructed from heavy timber and reinforced with wrought iron. He considered how the artisans and carpenters meticulously carved each panel with Gothic tracery, floral motifs, and religious iconography.

Four stories rose from the wagon's aft. They reminded Matthias of a ship's aftcastle, with each tier stacked vertically, each level set back slightly from the one beneath, creating the illusion of an enormous staircase. Open balconies framed by ornate balustrades were adorned with statues of saints and angels that peered down at the crowd. On the uppermost terrace, a commanding statue of Saint Michael, the archangel, stood poised with his sword raised, his wings spread wide as though ready to descend and smite evil. Just below, Saint Peter held the keys to Heaven in one hand, his expression severe, a reminder of the reckoning that awaited all souls.

Flanking the lower balconies, Gabriel the Archangel was rendered mid-step, holding a trumpet in one hand as if preparing to announce the call to judgment. Beside him, a statue of Saint Mary Magdalene stood with a jar of ointment at her feet, her hands clasped in repentance. The late afternoon sun's golden glow caught the gilded details of their halos, casting luminous reflections over the square. It was as if the entire Hierarchy of Angels had been deliberately caged for the journey to Bruges, arriving together on the same wagon.

Colossal wooden figures crafted by master puppeteers stood on the platform. Each puppet was controlled from above by an intricate network of pulleys, ropes, and counterweights all ingeniously concealed within the uppermost tier of the wagon's framework. The puppeteers manipulated these figures from behind the scenes, hidden among the carved wooden architecture of the aftcastle and buried beneath the stage flooring. Once set in motion, the giant figures appeared as living, animated beings.

An elaborate amplification system was fashioned out of copper tubes. The piping, masquerading as a web of vines, clung to the structure's exterior. At the top of the structure, the speaking tubes were capped with conical pieces made of wood and brass that resembled the flare of a trumpet's bell. These faced out to the crowd in every direction. To enhance the spectacle, the puppeteers would speak the play's dialogue into the tubes at the other end, their voices resonating through the bell-like ends, amplifying their voices. The effect gave the figures an otherworldly quality, as if the giant puppets spoke directly to the crowds below.

Crouched beneath the floor were musicians playing drums, lutes and bells in sync the puppets' movements. Matthias could see them through small, porthole-like windows between the wagon's enormous wheels.

He was so captivated by the movable stage and its mechanisms that it took him a moment to realize that François was nudging him for attention.

"You look like you've seen a miracle." François chuckled.

Matthias blinked. "The way they move, I've never seen anything like it."

Willem grinned, his voice brimming with excitement. "It's as if the giants are alive!"

Matthias turned to Willem, curious about what the boy did for a trade. "Willem, what is your trade, if I may ask?"

"I'm an apprentice for an artist, a painter. Mostly, I prepare canvases and mix pigments and sometimes assist in creating underdrawings for the master's works. In time, I'll take on my commissions and gain independence as a journeyman—that's my plan."

François interjected, "He loves what he does and speaks incessantly about his access to rare pigments and how challenging it is to capture light and shadow. He's a regular van Eyck," François said with a grin, clapping Willem on the back. "At least, that's what he'll tell you after a few ales."

Matthias returned his gaze to the wagon and its giants, then looked at François. "Imagine building something like that! Every detail, every pulley and rope hidden just so. I can only dream of working on a piece with so much art and skill."

"Well," François replied, placing a hand on Matthias' shoulder, "with that keen eye of yours, I'd say Bruges is the right place for you. Our craftsmen here could use someone with your appreciation for detail."

"Maybe even an artist like me," Willem said, grinning. "I can see it now—Matthias, the journeyman of Oudenaarde, designing the next great miracle of the square!"

Hope stirred in Matthias: the towering wagon, the artistry, the possibilities. Matthias lingered in his reverie. If Bruges could create such wonders, it would have a place for a craftsman like him.

"Let's not get ahead of ourselves, Willem. I'm a weaver by trade, but I'm willing to try anything and learn new skills if necessary as long as I can find work here."

Everyman

The giants loomed, their shadows fell,
And echoes tolled like judgment's knell.
A play unfolds, where deeds are bared,
With justice weighed, no soul is spared.
François, alert, the Canon spied,
His piercing gaze where secrets hide.
With Willem close, they faced the dread,
Of truths unspoken, fears unsaid.

François van Daele eyed Matthias with amusement as the journeyman took in the spectacle before him. Beside him, Willem watched the wagon and its shackled characters with awe and a slight hint of fear, even though he had witnessed this theater troupe several years in a row. The scene in the square, however, always managed to command attention.

François leaned slightly toward Matthias, his voice pitched low enough for Willem to overhear. "You know what this is, don't you?"

Matthias shook his head, his eyes still on the towering puppets and the black-robed figures moving like shadows among the machinery.

"The Summoning of Everyman," François explained, "is a morality play—how the high Father of Heaven sends a messenger to call every soul to account for their lives in this world."

Matthias tore his gaze from the stage, his brow furrowing.

"Every soul?"

"Everyman is a figure of us all," François continued, gesturing subtly toward the stage where the play's herald had begun his solemn recitation. "He learns how fleeting Strength, Beauty, and Fellowship are—how they all abandon him when it matters most. In the end, only Good Deeds remain to stand by his side before God."

Matthias blinked, digesting the words as he turned back to the stage. Willem shifted uneasily beside them, his expression caught between intrigue and unease.

François continued, "No one escapes their judgment day. No one." Then his gaze returned to the crowd, where Canon Henric van der Velde had yet to appear. François' chest tightened, the priest's eventual presence feeling as inevitable as the moral reckoning soon to unfold on the stage.

Now that the wagon had found its place in the square, a pair of grooms darted forward and took hold of the horses' reins. Short, sharp snorts escaped the horses as their manes flew, their heads jerking with restless energy, their flanks slick with sweat after the haul into town. One boy murmured soothingly as he unfastened the harnesses, bells jingling softly. The other tugged gently to lead the horses toward the stables, where fresh hay and water awaited. The boys' voices and the accompanying clip-clop-clang of tired iron-shod hooves against stone faded into the distance, leaving the square cloaked in an eerie, anticipatory silence.

The wagon waited expectantly, poised for the spectacle to begin. The puppeteers emerged from the scaffolding, their hooded black robes rising like smoke from a smoldering fire. They emerged with a purpose, sensing the moment was safe for their unearthly craft. Like demons surfacing from the depths, they waited for mortal eyes to vanish before revealing themselves.

With quick, practiced motions, they pulled levers, hoisted ropes, and cranked gears to transform the wagon into a living stage. The towering giants stirred, reborn; their imposing frames scarred the surrounding buildings in monstrous silhouettes, while beneath the floorboards, hidden from view, the musicians heightened the tension with a rapid, chaotic crescendo. The tempo surged, fierce and wild, until it broke with a thunderous drumbeat that shook the air.

And then—silence.

A human—not one of the giants on stage—appeared beside the wagon, slowly scanning the crowd. He prowled around the structure, peering into each person's face, not merely waiting for but demanding their attention. When the crowd settled, the man spoke:

> *I pray you all give your audience,*
> *And hear this matter with reverence,*
> *By figure a moral play:*
> *The Summoning of Everyman called it is,*
> *That of our lives and ending shows*
> *How transitory we be all day.*
> *This matter is wondrous precious,*
> *But the intent of it is more gracious,*
> *And sweet to bear away.*

The words rang out solemnly and deliberately, captivating François as though the giant puppets were speaking directly to him.

Ye think sin in the beginning full sweet,
Which in the end causeth thy soul to weep,
When the body lieth in clay.
Here shall you see how Fellowship and Jollity,
Both Strength, Pleasure, and Beauty
Will fade from thee as flower in May;
For ye shall hear how our Heavenly King
Calleth Everyman to a general reckoning:
Give audience, and hear what he doth say.

The rhythm of the lines and the gravity of their meaning sent a shiver through him. But then, a shift in the crowd's murmur jolted François back to reality. Just beyond the crowd's edge, a portly dark figure glided forward—a familiar presence that François immediately recognized, though he wished he hadn't. Canon Henric van der Velde.

François stiffened, his eyes darting cautiously over van der Velde's imposing frame and the gleaming ring of office on his thick finger. The man maneuvered through the crowd as if his attention was absorbed only by the performance. But François noticed how van der Velde's eyes scanned the gathering, lingering on some just long enough to make them feel scrutinized. All the while, his thick fingers toyed with the ring of office—a subtle yet potent reminder of the authority he wielded.

An icy pang shot through François as he nudged Willem, who remained engrossed in the play, oblivious to the tension growing beside him.

"Look," François whispered, his voice barely audible above the faint notes of the musicians. "Van der Velde."

Willem's eyes widened, his gaze snapping toward the priest. The Canon had just turned his head slightly, his eyes resting briefly on the two of them.

Willem's face blanched, and fear interrupted the awe that had gripped him moments before. His hand twitched at his side, and without thinking, François reached out, their fingers grazing in a fleeting touch. It wasn't a planned gesture, more instinct than intentional, but Willem's skin's warmth sent a jolt through him.

The contact lasted only a heartbeat—no more. But it carried an unspoken promise: I'm here. I won't leave you to face this alone.

Van der Velde's eyes spoke of a dark knowledge—of secrets best to conceal, a reminder of his power, a warning etched in his presence. He stopped short of them, his eyes, sharp and unyielding, fixed first on François, then Willem. For a moment, he said nothing, letting the weight of his gaze and the crowd's oblivious murmur stretch the tension between them.

"François," van der Velde said finally, his voice low, smooth but edged like a blade sheathed in silk. "Willem. A fine day for a play, wouldn't you agree?"

François swallowed, his throat dry. "Indeed, Father. The company is exceptional."

Van der Velde's lips curled into a smile that lacked warmth. His fingers resumed their slow, deliberate turn of the ring, and he leaned in just enough to lower his voice, excluding all but the two of them from his words. "The cloister is a sanctuary for reflection and prayer, not indiscretions to be shared with others no matter how trustworthy. Word travels quickly among these cobbled streets, as you well know."

Willem looked ready to crumble, but François held his composure, his voice steady though his heart raced. "We are always discreet, Father. Surely you understand the value of privacy."

Van der Velde's smile widened, though his eyes remained cold. "Privacy is a fleeting luxury, my son. But discretion? That is a virtue I trust you will embrace fully." He straightened, his tone shifting to something almost conversational. "Take care in your movements, both of you. Some would take joy in tearing down what they don't understand."

François' jaw tightened. "We appreciate your... guidance."

"Good," the Canon said, his tone as final as a slammed door. He cast one last, penetrating look between them before slipping back into the crowd.

François couldn't help but notice how his shadow stretched across the square, merging with the dark, towering, shadowed silhouettes cast by the giant puppets on stage. There was a chilling similarity—van der Velde's shadow loomed just as ominously, a reminder that his reach, like that of the grotesque figures, could fall over anyone it touched.

"He suspects someone knows," François aid, reaching for Willem's hand a second time, their fingers locking for the briefest moment before he let go. "But we'll be careful. We have to be."

Willem nodded, though his expression remained clouded. "What if we're followed? Or worse—if they already have?"

François squared his shoulders, his voice soft but firm. "Then we make sure they see nothing worth repeating."

The dark truths spoken on stage mimicked Henric's

warning, a figure who commanded dread as effortlessly as the towering giants before them. The booming drumbeat resumed, the words from the stage eerily suited to the moment:

"Ye think sin in the beginning full sweet,

Which in the end causeth thy soul to weep..."

François let his hand fall back to his side, the absence of Willem's touch somehow louder than the lines echoing through the square. François thought bitterly of how far van der Velde's authority extended beyond his secluded quarters.

François clapped Matthias on the shoulder, forcing a smile as if the gesture could shake off the weight of the Canon's warning. "So, where are you staying while you're here?"

Matthias shifted uneasily, scratching his neck. "I...haven't found a place just yet."

François exchanged a glance with Willem. "Ah, then you're in luck. We know a place nearby—Saint Jan's Hospital—where you can have a roof over your head, a bed for your body, and a meal for your soul."

Willem added, "When you're settled, we'll take you to The Bear. Show you where the real hospitality is."

Matthias smiled, his gratitude evident. The promise of a warm meal and good company was enticing, so he followed them out of the square and down a narrow street. The echoes of drums and revelry faded, giving way to a quieter atmosphere. Matthias fell behind and glanced back toward the square. He was aware that François had slowed his pace to join him. "François," Matthias said, his voice low enough to draw him closer. "That priest...I saw him earlier today."

François stiffened, the weight of Matthias' words settling between them like a stone. His mouth tightened into a hard line, but he said nothing, waiting for Matthias to continue.

"I noticed him during the Mass," Matthias admitted, his voice uneasy. "When I returned to my place after Communion... his eyes followed me."

François turned toward Willem; his eyes confirmed he shared François' unease.

Matthias hesitated. Even in the dim light, François could see the flush of discomfort creeping up his face. "I don't think I'm imagining it," Matthias murmured. "The way he looked at me—" His voice faltered, his gaze dropping to the cobblestones. "It wasn't the kind of attention a man of the cloth should give anyone. It was..." He fell silent.

François' jaw tightened. "You're not imagining it," he said grimly. His voice was barely above a whisper, but its conviction left no room for doubt. "Henric van der Velde doesn't watch people for nothing. There's always a reason—his reason."

Willem jolted, his movement betraying his fear. He glanced over his shoulder, expecting van der Velde's imposing figure to emerge from the shadows. "All the more reason to stay out of his path," he said tightly.

François nodded but kept his gaze fixed ahead. "Best to be wary around him," François coldly warned.

As they walked on, François couldn't shake the gnawing realization that the Canon's appetite was insatiable. This hunger sought out more than just him and Willem, reaching for anyone who strayed too close.

The Bear

The Bear's warm hearth, a ruddy glow,
Where laughter rose, the embers low.
François and Willem, bonds held tight,
Found haven in the tavern's light.
Yet shadows danced through amber flame,
And watchful eyes played quiet games.
Lode's sharp gaze, like embered stone,
Concealed a threat yet still unknown.

François hesitated in the doorway of The Bear, a cozy inn nestled at the corner of Geauwwerkersstraat and Vlamingstraat, just beside the bustling bourse. Anticipating a good meal, he took in the familiar sight of wooden beams stretching across the ceiling, darkened by years of smoke and warmth. Every inch of wall space told a story—portraits and engravings, some faded, others surprisingly vibrant, depicting solemn milkmaids, the shoreline dunes of Wenduin, or the forests of Eecklo. Flames flickered in the large stone fireplace, embers crackling as they cast a pulsing red hue over the tables and the faces of local revelers.

Behind him, Willem, his oldest friend, nudged his shoulder, snapping François out of his reverie. With a nod, François stepped inside, followed by Willem and his newest friend, Matthias. Together, they crossed the room, the air thick with the aroma of stews and roasting meats wafting from beyond the hearth.

He and Willem had been coming here since they could

venture out on their own. The Bear quickly had become their favorite spot, where they could retreat from the bustle of the streets. Today, after witnessing the solemnity of the Procession of the Holy Blood, the spectacle of a morality play in the square, and the tense encounter with van der Velde, they had brought Matthias to share a meal in this familiar haven.

The innkeeper, Pieter Van de Steen, greeted François with a cheerful nod and a robust laugh. Stocky and broad-shouldered, Pieter moved through the room with practiced ease, balancing the demands of a bustling inn. His rolled-up sleeves revealed muscled forearms toned by years of hauling casks and heavy bags of produce and flour, his sturdy leather apron marked with the streaks of a day's labor. His wife, Margriet, bustled between tables, carrying pots of stew, platters of spit-roasted meats, and pitchers of ale.

François noticed the young worker near the bar, a wiry lad named Lode. He carried wood for the fireplace with nervous energy. His patched cloak clung tightly around him, shielding him from more than the room's chill. The frayed edges of his faded doublet and the dingy collar of his hastily donned linen shirt completed his furtive demeanor.

Lode glanced up briefly, his eyes darting toward François and Willem, only to flit away as though he'd been caught doing something wrong. François sensed the boy's unease—a wariness that was out of place. Had he wronged Lode unintentionally? The thought lingered, nagging at him as he observed the boy's practiced hesitancy, the way he glanced over his shoulder as if expecting trouble or fearing he'd be dismissed from his job.

When François reached the table, he unhooked his bowl,

eating knife, and simple drinking cup from his belt and set them down with a clink. These modest tools awaited whatever the innkeepers might provide. François settled into the room and caught Willem's eye, and a quiet glance passed between them—a shared relief at being back in their trusted haven.

François reached across the table, his fingers skimming briefly against Willem's wrist, barely noticeable yet charged with meaning. It might have been mistaken for a fleeting accident, but François knew otherwise.

Willem smirked grimly. For a moment, the bustle of the inn faded into the background—the scrape of chairs, the clink of mugs, the hum of laughter—all muted by the quiet understanding that passed between them.

"It's good to be back," François murmured.

Willem nodded, his thumb grazed the edge of François' sleeve, then pulled back. "It is," he replied, the warmth in his tone carrying more weight than the spoken words.

Margriet arrived at their table to take their order. She wore a sage green wool dress, the fitted bodice shaping her frame while the full skirt swayed with her movement. A linen apron tied snugly at her waist bore the marks of a busy day, and a wool shawl was draped loosely over her shoulders to guard against the lingering outside chill when the inn's door was open to let in customers. Her headscarf, tied neatly, framed her face, and though her brow glistened from the work of a long day, her eyes sparkled with warmth as she greeted the men. "Well, if it isn't François and his band of merry men," she said, wiping her hands on her apron and eyeing Matthias with a chuckle. "And I see you've brought a fresh face. Don't worry, lad—we don't bite, not even the green ones."

Matthias shifted in his seat, a sheepish grin creeping across his face, while François and Willem exchanged a knowing look. The innkeeper's wife, Margriet, folded her arms, one eyebrow arched expectantly.

"So, what'll it be? Stew's hot and thick today—rabbit and root vegetables with spice to keep you warm. Or perhaps the roast? It just came off the spit, tender and dripping as it should be. And I've got fresh, warm bread if you need more to fill those bellies."

François, unable to hide his smile, nodded appreciatively. "The stew sounds fine, and maybe some of that bread to go with it," he replied.

"Stew it is, then," Willem agreed, looking around as the savory aroma of roasting meat and herbs wafted through the room.

Matthias, still wide-eyed, nodded vigorously. "The stew, yes, please."

Margriet returned briskly, carrying a hefty iron pot cradled in one hand and a basket of fresh bread tucked under her arm. Setting the pot down on the table with a practiced thud, she reached for a ladle hanging from her apron. The savory aroma of rabbit and root vegetable stew filled the air as she stirred the contents, steam curling upward.

"There you are, lads," she said, ladling generous portions into the bowls they had placed before her. "Rich and hearty rabbit stew with spice to keep the chill away. And the bread just left the hearth, perfect for sopping up every last drop."

François leaned forward, his bowl now brimming with the rich broth and chunks of tender rabbit, carrots, turnips, and onions. The scent of herbs—thyme, parsley, and cloves—added to the inn's warmth. He broke off a piece of bread, its crust cracking from the force, and dipped it into the stew, savoring the first bite. "This is wonderful, Margriet," François said. "You've outdone yourself."

"I agree," Willem added, halfway through his first piece of bread. "Stew like this could make a man forget the cold outside."

Matthias speared a tender piece of rabbit with the pointed tip of his eating knife, savoring it before breaking off a chunk of bread to sop up the thick broth. He brought the bowl to his lips to slurp the rest of the savory liquid, letting out a satisfied sigh. "It's perfect," he mumbled through a full mouth, earning a laugh from Margriet.

"Well then, eat up and keep your bellies full," she said with a grin, turning back toward the kitchen. "No use letting good stew go to waste."

As the food's warmth settled over them, François noticed Lode standing rigidly in front of the hearth, his piercing glare fixed on their table. The jitteriness that usually defined him had hardened into something darker; his unblinking, cold gaze darted between each of the men.

François' smile faltered as Lode's eyes met his—keen and piercing, glinting like shards of amber in the firelight. The intensity of his gaze was unsettling, feral, as though he were sizing François up, not as a companion but as something more ambiguous. His sharp scowl twisted the hearth's glow into something harsh, the flickering shadows on the walls seeming to ripple and snap like the bristle of fur in an unseen wind.

The easy comfort of The Bear thinned, just for a moment, revealing an edge François hadn't noticed before—an edge that hinted at something untamed. Lode's shoulders hunched forward like a predator poised to pounce.

The moment passed, and Lode's sharp eyes slid away as he returned to his task with quiet precision. Yet the impact of the brief encounter lingered, as though he'd left an unseen shadow in his wake—a faint growl of tension in the air, unspoken but undeniable.

Lode's Betrayal

In shadowed halls, a bitter heart,
Let envy's flame its venom start.
Lode watched their joy, his shame did burn,
To darkness deep his soul did turn.
A letter scribed with trembling hand,
Its cruel intent, a ruthless brand.
Upon the door, his hammer fell,
Its echo rang the night's dark knell.

Lode pressed his back against The Bear's cool stone wall. His heart raced as he watched François, Willem, and their friend laughing, drinking, and basking in the inn's warmth. His gaze narrowed as he noted the camaraderie between them. He wondered if the newcomer was like them, too. His stomach twisted, bitterness welling up inside him.

It wasn't the first time he'd felt that burning jealousy. A few months earlier, on one of his nightly haunts through the dim streets of Bruges, he had stumbled upon François and Willem leaving van der Velde's private quarters. Cloaked in shadow, he watched them emerge, their heads close together, their laughter low but unmistakable. Lode flattened himself against a wall, his breath caught in his throat.

They spoke in hushed tones, their figures outlined by the faint light spilling from a high, arched window. François' hands carved through the air fervently, and Willem nodded, his youthful face alight with admiration. They shared a secret bond that drew them together and away from the rest of the world.

What could they have been doing behind the Canon's closed doors? What privileges had they secured that were denied to the rest of them? The more he considered what could be going on between the three of them, the more his questions multiplied, each one more poisonous than the last, adding to his confusion and vulnerability.

He had stood there for what felt like hours, his thoughts a cyclone of suspicion, envy, and something darker—something bitter and twisted that he could neither name nor banish. His heart raced, his palms were slick with sweat, and his mind was a battleground of conflicting emotions. Whatever was happening unsettled him profoundly.

They had privilege, while he was left to scrape by in the shadows. Why were they worthy of such attention? Each question festered, turning his jealousy into an obsession.

A few days after observing the two men, Lode asked for an audience with van der Velde. Once granted and standing before the man, he stammered an innocent plea, appealing for the Canon's guidance. He spoke of his troubled past, the jobs lost through no fault of his own—or so he claimed—and his desperate need for stability. "You're a man of infinite power and grace, Canon. Someone like me could thrive under your protection."

The conversation stalled, and van der Velde's cold gaze beaconed more than just words. In a bold move, Lode leaned closer, his hands clawing the edge of van der Velde's desk as if to anchor himself. A smile—hesitant, coy—crept onto his face. "I'd be loyal to you, Canon," he murmured, his voice a low, intimate timbre that surprised even himself. "In every way you needed."

Van der Velde's expression darkened, his lips curling in disdain. Silence stretched between them while Lode waited for a response; when none came, he pressed on, his desperation overriding all caution and propriety. He reached out just enough for his fingers to graze van der Velde's sleeve—a gesture of gratitude, or so he told himself, though the intent behind it was far more reckless.

"You dare to think someone of my station would stoop to filth like you?" van der Velde spat, recoiling as though Lode's touch had burned him. His voice sliced through the air, sharp as a blade. "Leave now and pray for your wretched soul."

Lode's cheeks burned with humiliation as the Canon's rejection cut deep. He had gambled everything on this moment—his dignity and hopes of survival—and been rejected.

Now, as he stood in the darkened corridor at The Bear, the laughter at François' table grated against him like grinding stone. François and Willem glided through life untouched by the struggles that plagued him. If they could charm van der Velde's favor, why should he be condemned for trying to do the same?

His fingers spasmed into fists, his nails cutting into his palms. They would all pay for this injustice.

In recent weeks, he'd pieced together whispered rumors and snatches of conversation, knowing what the townsfolk had started to murmur, rumors that carried a dangerous charge, encircling François, Willem, and others in an illicit ring of misbehavior and defiance of law and nature. Though it wasn't his business, their secret threatened everyone connected to it, and Lode couldn't shake the growing dread.

He needed to act to bring justice and clarity to the fog of rumors. He thought of the letter he'd meticulously written in the dark of his room, which he hoped would expose the truth and protect the community.

"Lode, get back to work," came a voice. It was the innkeeper calling him back to his chores. He hurried to the hearth with a fresh load of wood, carefully avoiding François' glance. His cheeks grew hot from the fire's heat that now fused with his anger. The letter's words swirled in his mind as he knelt before the hearth: *Unholy acts within the Canon Henric van der Velde's walls, practiced by those you least expect.* He imagined the townsfolk gathering in front of the notice nailed to the town hall door, the shock that would fill them with righteous rage.

He stole another glance at François, the calm smile, the ease with which he lived each day. For all the whispers he'd heard of François' devotion and good name, the weight of their actions—secrets hidden in the shadowed cloister of van der Velde's private quarters—grew heavier by the day.

With the fire stoked, he straightened, catching the glimmer of laughter at François' table. This would be the night he made his move, the night to save the town and reveal François and Willem for who they were—sodomites.

The evening wore on, and the last patrons stumbled out, leaving The Bear in a calm, drowsy quiet. Lode scrubbed the vacated tables with rough strokes, each scrape sharpening his resolve. As he finished, he grabbed his worn coat and slipped his hand into the pocket, feeling his letter's smooth, folded edges—a promise and a threat. He steadied himself and took a deep breath before picking up the hammer and nails he'd tucked beneath the bar.

"Good night, Pieter, Good night, Margriet. I'll see you tomorrow," he called out as he left.

The door creaked shut behind him as he stepped into the night. Vlamingstraat stretched into the dark, its damp stones glistening under the moonlight. His breath escaped in short, foggy puffs. In the distance the Belfry loomed. Even in shadow, its facade was imposing—a fitting witness to his task. He pulled his coat tighter and set out, his boots echoing against the slick paving stones as he slipped through narrow alleys toward the square.

Lode's pace quickened once he entered Market Square, The Belfry rising before him like a stone sentinel etched against the Flemish sky. He turned onto a passageway into Burg Square, and there stopped before the Stadhuis, Bruges' town hall. Its pale limestone facade was adorned with Bruges' coat of arms and heraldic shields. Intricately carved statues of historical figures were set into niches, and soaring Gothic windows framed by delicate tracery reflected Bruges' civic pride and wealth during its golden age as a center of trade and commerce more than a hundred years ago, in 1421.

Fingers trembling, he pulled the folded letter from his coat and stopped. He heard a series of soft metallic clinks and a gentle creak nearby. He froze, his heart pounding. He scanned his surroundings and discovered the sounds emanated from a hanging shop sign. He shook his head and calmed his nerves, satisfied that he was alone.

He retrieved the letter and held it flat against the heavy wood. With a single, deliberate motion, he raised the hammer and drove a nail through the parchment with more force than needed. The sharp thud echoed, resonating like a crack of thunder. It startled his ears and sent a sharp pain through his hand and up his forearm.

He worked methodically, each nail anchoring the accusations more firmly into place. The faint rustle of the paper straining against the night breeze unnerved him, like whispers on the edge of hearing. A strange and layered feeling washed over him as he hammered the final nail—relief, anger, and an uneasy fear that prickled at the back of his neck.

Lode stepped back, surveying his work. Outwardly, the letter was innocuous, yet its contents were lethal, the words cutting deeper than a blade. A stillness settled over him. In that moment, the weight of his past was replaced by a fragile sense of purpose, a sacrifice made in the name of justice. He felt the warmth of grace touch his soul as if nailing truth to the door might anchor him to salvation. He flexed his hands, the faint tremor from hammering still lingering in his fingers.

As his boots echoed through the empty streets, Lode couldn't shake the feeling that he'd set something far greater into motion.

Matthias' Dilemma

Through Bruges' still streets Matthias crept,
Through alleys dark, where secrets slept.
He saw the boy with venom's aim,
A parchment nailed, a soul to shame.
The words he read, a city's pain,
Their honor bent by Lode's disdain.
Though fear did clutch his racing heart,
He vowed to play his loyal part.

Just outside The Bear's entrance on Vlamingstraat, Matthias lingered in the shadows, the evening chill burrowing through his coat. The glow of lantern light reflected off the canal, casting wobbling patterns over buildings. Something about Lode seemed amiss all evening—the furtive glances, the way he bristled whenever François and Willem laughed together. Now, with the streets empty and silent, Matthias' curiosity had hardened into suspicion.

A door creaked open at the rear of The Bear, and Lode slipped out. Matthias barely dared to breathe as he pressed himself against the rough wall, watching the boy disappear into the alley. He momentarily considered returning to his lodgings at Saint Jan's Hospital, dismissing his unease as unfounded. But there was something in Lode's purposeful gait—something too deliberate to ignore. Matthias decided to follow.

The streets were quiet except for the faint wind whistling

around the eaves. Matthias crept from shadow to shadow, careful to keep his steps light. In the short time since his arrival in Bruges, with the help of François and Willem, he had learned to navigate the city by using the seven gates and numerous windmills that dotted the circular perimeter of the fortified town, whose defensive walls and network of canals, doubling as a moat, encircled its heart like a protective ring.

Ahead, Lode moved swiftly, his slim figure melding with the darkened streets. Matthias lost sight of him momentarily as the boy disappeared past a row of market stalls lining Breidelstraat. Panic swelled in his chest as he hurried forward, sticking close to the shadows.

The narrow street opened onto Burg Square, and Matthias slowed as the grand silhouette of the Stadhuis loomed ahead. He passed under an overhanging sign swinging on chains in the light wind. The sign read: "The Leathern Sole." The cobbler's shop was tucked into the corner of the square, its recessed doorway offering just enough cover. Matthias crouched down and watched Lode take the steps to the town hall two at a time.

With quick, deliberate movements, Matthias watched as the boy pulled a folded parchment from his coat and nailed it to the heavy wood. The sharp thuds of the hammer echoed through the empty square, and Matthias flinched with each strike. When Lode stepped back to inspect his work, Matthias squinted, trying to make out the words on the parchment, but the distance and dim light made it impossible.

When the deed was done, Lode slipped across the square, returning to the passageway toward Market Square and out of sight. Matthias darted toward the door, his pulse pounding in his ears. He hesitated as he reached for the parchment, the coarse paper crinkling under his fingers. His chest tightened—what if someone saw him? But the need to know burned brighter than his fear. Carefully, he leaned closer, the faint light from a nearby lantern illuminating the damning words:

To the people of Bruges,

Let it be known that the common folk of Bruges, and even those held in esteem, are tainted by the criminal sin and crime of sodomy, a stain that pollutes our city.

Among the worst offenders are François van Daele and Willem de Clerck, who, under the guise of respectability, have long reveled in these unnatural acts as though their reputations granted them impunity. Yet, their dark deeds bring our people nothing but shame and dishonor.

I write this not to slander without cause but to warn the good citizens of Bruges of the hidden sins corrupting our fair city. Let this knowledge serve as both a warning and a call to vigilance that we may cleanse our city of such depravity and restore it to honor.

A Concerned Burgher

Matthias placed his palm against the door beside the letter, his head resting against the cold wood. His pulse roared in his ears as the weight of the words sank in. He thought of François' quiet strength and Willem's warm laughter—their companionship had been a rare kindness since his arrival in Bruges. Such cruelty was not their due. His hand itched to rip the letter down, but his resolve faltered. What if he were seen? What if tearing it down only drew more attention?

The cold venom of the letter seeped into Matthias' bones. How could Lode do this? Out of loyalty to François and Willem, Matthias wanted to shield them from the accusations, unwilling to feed the growing rumors about Bruges' so-called "disease." But fear tugged at him. Who else might secretly conspire if Lode was bold enough to post this publicly? He backed away, torn between rage and helplessness.

The sharp blare of a night watchman's horn shattered the silence, causing Matthias to jump and stumble back into the safety of the Leathern Sole's entryway as the watchman stepped into the square. The man raised his lantern, its light swinging lazily across the cobblestones as he climbed the steps to the town hall. Matthias held his breath as the watchman scanned the door, his gaze focused on the newly posted letter. After a long moment, the man sounded midnight and continued his nightly rounds, marking the hours, checking the security of shops and guild halls, and looking for mischievous behavior.

Matthias exhaled shakily, retreating from the square. His mind raced as he walked, the now familiar streets blurring around him. He had failed to take down Lode's proclamation, but its words burned in his memory, each sharper and crueler than the last. He knew he had to warn François and Willem.

Matthias retreated from Burg Square and roamed the lace-like pattern of streets until he crossed a narrow stone bridge, his footsteps percussive against its timbered flooring, the canal's gurgle barely audible in the stillness. He passed the Church of Our Lady, its spire piercing the night sky, the silhouette reassuring and ominous. The street was quiet as he reached the stone walls of Saint Jan's Hospital, the scent of damp stone and faint herbs mingling in the air. Once through the hospital's gates, his pace quickened, the weight of his purpose pressing heavily on his chest. Once inside, the hospital felt like a sanctuary as it had earlier that day when François and Willem brought him there as a temporary refuge. But now, it felt more like a hiding place—a safe harbor before an approaching storm, the faint scent of herbs and linen doing little to calm his nerves.

Matthias slumped onto the cot assigned to him, the weight of the evening pressing down like the stone walls around him. He thought of The Bear's warm glow, the laughter shared over bread and stew, and his bond with his friends. They needed to know what Lode had done. He would seek them out tomorrow, perhaps starting back at The Bear. Pieter and Margriet might know where to find them.

His resolve hardened as he stared at the darkened ceiling. Matthias vowed to stand by François and Willem in whatever storm was brewing in Bruges. They had given him kindness and a place to belong. Now, it was his turn to protect them—even if it meant stepping into the storm himself.

Loyalty

Within The Bear's warm fire's glow,
A vow was made where shadows grow.
For François bold and Willem true,
Matthias swore their trials he'd view.
Betrayal's sting and whispers' roar,
Lode's venom grew, a fest'ring sore.
Yet loyalty burned, a fragile flame,
To face the dark, to bear the blame.

After a day spent searching for work and worrying about François and Willem, Matthias stepped into The Bear as dusk crept over Bruges. The clatter of mugs and the low murmur of regulars' chatter greeted him, softened by the delicate notes of a lutist strumming in the corner. The inn's smoky warmth should have been a comfort, but the sounds faded into the background for Matthias. He scanned the room briefly, finding no sign of his friends, and made his way to the end of the long table, his rust-colored doublet blending into the shadows.

Mud clods clung to his boots—a stubborn reminder of the hurried journey here. His fingers absently adjusted the knitted scarf at his neck, but his thoughts circled back to Lode's letter. The condemning words had been hammered to the city hall door for all to see, accusing François and Willem of unspeakable acts. No matter how hard he tried, Matthias couldn't unsee the sharp, black ink slashing across the page like a wound. He had no reason to believe the accusations, but the words burrowed into his mind. Could they have misstepped somehow? A careless jest, a look held too long—anything that might have been twisted into this monstrosity? No. It wasn't possible. Though he'd only met François and Willem a day before, Matthias felt sure of their character. Their easy camaraderie and openness had left him with a sense of trust. If anyone could speak the truth plainly, it was François and Willem.

"Don't worry, love, they'll be here. They're always here."

Margriet, the innkeeper's wife, approached with her usual calm presence, her sage-green dress swishing softly as she set a fresh mug of ale in front of him. Clean linen peeked under her flour-dusted apron, and the shawl draped over her shoulders spoke of practicality, not luxury.

"You look like a lad with the world's weight on his shoulders." She placed a basket of bread rolls on the table, their golden crusts glistening. "Let me guess—you have important news to share?"

Matthias forced a small smile. "You could say that."

Margriet chuckled, wiping her hands on her apron. "The Bear's seen its share of important meetings over the years. Pieter and I used to think it was just a place for hungry locals and travelers, but sometimes I wonder if these walls don't hold on to secrets."

Her words tugged at Matthias' curiosity, pulling him briefly from his reverie. "Did you and Pieter always run this place?"

"Oh, heavens no," she replied with a laugh. "We took it over from Pieter's uncle after his debts nearly closed the doors. It wasn't easy, but we made it a refuge again. Pieter likes to say the walls are ours now, though sometimes I wonder if they still whisper about what they've seen."

Her gaze drifted toward the bar, where Lode stacked mugs with his usual nervous energy. "Take that one, for instance. We gave him a place here after he'd run out of chances elsewhere."

Matthias followed her gaze. Lode moved with a jittery rhythm, glancing over his shoulder every few seconds as though expecting to be caught. "What kind of trouble?"

Margriet shrugged, her smile tinged with sadness. "The kind that follows a man who can't stay still long enough to build trust. He stirs the pot too much—always hearing more than he should, always saying too much or too little. But he works hard when he sets his mind to it."

Matthias frowned. "Do you trust him?"

Margriet hesitated, the silence between them stretching taut. "I want to," she said at last. "But Lode…he's slippery. He works hard, but he's always watching. Always waiting."

The creak of the door drew her attention, and her face brightened. "Well, there you are! Your friends never miss a good meal."

Heads turned when François and Willem crossed the planked floor to the table, and the air in the room shifted with their arrival. Conversations faltered, and the soft murmur of the inn grew uneasy like a tide pulling away before a storm.

A man near the fire paused mid-drink, lowering his mug to mutter something to his companion. The other man's eyes darted toward François and Willem, then away, as if the sight of them burned.

At the bar, a pair of women whispered behind their hands,

one shaking her head sharply, the other glancing back with pity—or perhaps disdain.

As François and Willem passed a group of regulars hunched over their dice game, one of the players snorted audibly. "Seems they've made time to crawl out from under the Canon's skirts," he muttered, loud enough to carry. The table erupted in low, cruel laughter.

Willem's stride faltered momentarily, the corner of his jaw tightening, but he forced himself onward. François, however, kept his gaze fixed ahead. His hand settled on the hilt of the eating knife at his belt, fingers curling around it with nervous energy.

Matthias felt guilt as they sat. Around them, the muted chatter resumed, though not without the occasional sideways glance or barely concealed smirk.

Matthias noticed Willem's exhaustion and François' fidgeting with his mug. Gathering his courage, Matthias leaned forward.

"François, Willem…I need to tell you something. Something serious."

He told them about Lode's letter, the accusations nailed to the city hall door. The shock on their faces was immediate. François clenched his fists, his knuckles white as he gripped the table. "If my father hears of this…" His voice trailed off, panic flashing across his face.

Willem, usually composed, looked momentarily lost, his hand resting on François' arm to steady him. "It's not just about us," Willem murmured. "My mother… the shame of it…"

François' gaze darted around the room, taking in the furtive glances and lowered voices, and understanding dawned.

"So that's why..." he said quietly, his voice bitter. "The looks. The whispers when we came in. They've read it, haven't they? Or at least heard the rumors."

Willem nodded grimly, his jaw tightening. "They don't need proof. The letter is enough for them to decide what we are." His voice dropped further. "We're already guilty in their eyes."

Matthias leaned in. "Lode's words are vile, but they're only that—words. Anyone who knows you will see through them."

Willem gave a weak smile. "You have too much faith in this town."

"Faith?" François interjected, his voice tight. "Today at the tailor's, they handed me my coat and said they wouldn't mend it. There was no explanation, just a cold look. The whispers have already started."

Matthias looked between them, confusion growing. "But they're not true, are they? Lode twisted something, didn't he?"

François glanced at Willem, who shifted uncomfortably. "Matthias," Willem began, his voice low, "not all of it is false."

Matthias froze, his hands gripping the edge of the table. "What are you saying?"

François leaned in, guilt heavy in his gaze. "We've... we've been to van der Velde's quarters. More times than we should have. It wasn't just errands and messages." He hesitated, then added, "At first, it was harmless. He asked for help with records and small favors—favors we couldn't refuse."

Matthias stared at them, his chest tightening. "You mean..."

Willem's voice cracked. "We were desperate, Matthias.

François' father's debts, my mother's failing health—we had no other way to survive." He swallowed hard. "The Canon made promises. He said he could help us. And he did...but there was a price."

François sighed bitterly. "Lode knows just enough to make his accusations stick. He saw us coming and going from van der Velde's quarters. He heard things and guessed the rest."

The weight of their words settled over Matthias like a stone. His mind raced, but the sharp crackle of the fire silenced him. Around them, the low murmur of the Bear's regulars shifted. Matthias noticed glances in their direction—furtive, troubled looks from patrons. A pair of older men whispered to each other, their eyes darting toward François and Willem. At the bar, a woman turned her back abruptly, shaking her head.

"They're watching us," Matthias murmured, his voice barely audible.

Willem followed his gaze and paled. "It's already begun."

François clenched his fists, knuckles white against the worn wood of the table. "If my father hears of this..." His voice broke, and he looked away.

Willem reached for François' arm, steadying him. "It's not just about us," he whispered. "It's our families. The shame, the fallout—it will destroy them."

Matthias leaned in, his voice urgent. "Then we have to fight this. Somehow, we have to stop Lode before it spreads further."

François gave a bitter laugh. "Stop him? The damage is already done. Even if we silence him, van der Velde holds the strings. Lode is just a puppet."

Willem nodded grimly. "The Canon's power reaches

further than you know, Matthias. People fear him, even those who whisper behind our backs now. They'll look the other way if he demands it."

The door to the Bear creaked open, admitting a new customer and drawing half the room's attention. Matthias' stomach churned at the sound, but his eyes were pulled instead to the bar. Lode stepped forward from the shadows near the hearth, his movements deliberate, his gaze sweeping across the patrons. His eyes lingered on their table for a heartbeat too long, a thin, satisfied smile curling his lips before he turned back toward the mugs he had been stacking.

Matthias' stomach churned. "Lode... he's here."

François' jaw tightened, his eyes burning with anger. "He always is."

They studied each other's faces, their bond heavier now under the weight of shared secrets. The warmth of the Bear felt distant, replaced by the iron shadow of van der Velde's power and the communal whispers that would only grow louder.

Misstep

In alleys dark, their scheme took flight,
With coin exchanged beneath the night.
With Klaas and Bram, the trap was set,
To bind the two in shadow's net.
But greed betrayed the plan they wove,
The hunter snared, their truth unrove.
François and Willem, bruised but free,
Watched as Lode faced his decree.

Lode removed his apron and let it drop on the stairs in the darkness behind the bar. This was the moment he'd been waiting for. He'd posted his accusatory letter the night before, and now all he needed was someone to help bring them in for arrest.

He slid out of The Bear through the back door and began running. In all his planning, he hadn't thought about how to bring the two men to the authorities. François and Willem alone could be overpowered with the help of one or two others, but their friend Matthias complicated matters. He was strong, quick to act, and fiercely loyal, a combination that could tip the balance in a fight. The thought of a confrontation made Lode uneasy, but he couldn't rule out the possibility.

Lode paused to catch his breath, his mind racing. He had connections among Bruges' less reputable denizens—the kind who lurked in shadows eager to curry favor with Lode if it promised a profit in return. Often seen around The Bear, they listened for rumors, always seeking an advantage. Ruffians and dock workers haunted the fringes of the law, ready to sell their loyalty for a price. Lode planned to enlist one or two of them to help him bring in François and Willem, hoping the silver stuiver he'd found while sweeping up the floors at the tavern late one night would be enough to pay his accomplices.

He hadn't ventured far when he spotted two men leaning against a corner building leading onto Market Square, their postures loose and easy but their eyes focused and hard. They were familiar faces—ruffians who haunted this part of Bruges, always listening for a whisper of opportunity. He recognized the taller one, a well-muscled fellow named Klaas, who had a penchant for sniffing out trouble, and his stocky companion, Bram, a dockworker with heavy fists and a reputation for looking the other way if the price was right.

Lode hesitated but took a deep breath, walking confidently toward them."Evening, gentlemen," he said, lowering his voice to a conspiratorial tone. Klaas and Bram exchanged glances before skeptically eyeing Lode.

"Pleasant evening to you, lad," Klaas said, his eyes glinting in the dim light—sharp and calculating, like a predator sizing up its prey. His posture was deceptively relaxed, but there was a coiled readiness about him as though he might spring at Lode at the slightest provocation. "What brings you prowling around at this hour?"

Lode glanced over his shoulder, then leaned in. "I've got a job for you. A simple one," he said, reaching into his pocket and pulling out the silver stuiver, letting it gleam in the dim light. The two men's eyes fixed on the coin, hungry and intrigued.

Bram crossed his arms, his gaze narrowing. "We don't get out of bed for a coin," he muttered, but Lode held his ground.

Lode fidgeted, his fingers tapping the coin's edge as if trying to summon courage. His eyes darted toward Klaas and Bram, gauging their reactions like a subordinate watching for the alpha's approval.

"There's more where that came from if you're willing to help me," Lode said, lowering his voice even further. "I need you to handle two men—nothing drastic, just hold them until the authorities arrive."

Klaas raised an eyebrow, his sharp eyes assessing the offer, while Bram shifted his weight, his eyes flicking between his co-conspirator and the silver coin. He stayed close to Klaas; his loyalty tied not to trust but to the chance of a larger share of whatever spoils might come.

Lode forced a smile, raising the coin higher to catch their attention. "You'll get this now and the rest after. All I need is for you to ensure they don't get away. Just rough them up if they resist," Lode said, his voice dropping lower. He glanced around again. "These two are dangerous and need to be dealt with. If you're not up to it, I'll find someone else."

Despite his outward confidence, Lode's nervous tone betrayed him as the weakest link in the pack. Klaas raised an eyebrow, his sharp eyes assessing the offer, while Bram leaned forward slightly, the silver coin reflecting in his wide, unblinking eyes. His fingers twitched at his side as if imagining the prize's weight in his hand. He licked his lips before glancing toward Klaas, his hunger momentarily tempered by the need for his co-conspirator's approval.

Before Klaas could signal his agreement, Bram snatched

the coin from Lode's grasp. "We'll do it," he said, tucking the stuiver into his fist. "But if this goes sideways, it'll be you that we'll be after."

Lode nodded, swallowing his unease. "Fine. We'll station ourselves by The Bear until they leave. Just… be ready."

They waited in a hidden nook off the alley by The Bear. It wasn't long before François, Willem, and Matthias emerged. Lode's crew looked to him for the signal to proceed. Seeing the trio idly standing and saying their goodbyes spurred their eagerness to act, but Lode gestured for them to stay put, telling them he couldn't risk being recognized.

A moment later, Matthias parted ways with François and Willem, heading southwest down Vlamingstraat toward his lodgings at Saint Jan's Hospital. His footsteps echoed softly on the cobblestones, fading into the quiet night as he disappeared into the dimly lit street. Behind him, François and Willem remained near The Bear, left alone and vulnerable in the shadowed entrance. Unseen in the darkness, Lode watched, his patience rewarded. He had been waiting for this moment—the opportunity to strike.

The alley was awkwardly still as Lode and his accomplices remained hidden, but they were close enough to see the boys standing before the tavern. Klaas and Bram twitched with impatience, and their restlessness was evident.

François and Willem could be heard talking in low tones as they set off down the cobblestone street, their steps echoing softly in the quiet night. They headed opposite Matthias, who had veered off toward the main square. Unbeknownst to them, their path brought them closer to the shadowed passage where Lode, Klaas, and Bram lay in wait.

Lode gestured for his accomplices to wait, his voice tight with anticipation. "I'll stay here. They know who I am. No point in them spotting me and ruining the whole thing."

The three waited silently, suspicious of each other like restless predators forced to share the same hunting ground. Klaas' eyes shifted to the street while Bram rocked impatiently, his fingers tapping against his thigh.

When François and Willem neared, Lode's accomplices nodded and moved into the street as one, their coordination instinctive as they advanced on François and Willem, who had slowed as they entered the quieter lane leading to their homes.

Klaas lunged first, swift and deliberate, his hands closing around François with the unerring precision of a hunter locking onto its quarry. The opening salvo shattered the alley's quiet as Bram advanced on Willem.

Despite his size, Bram's movements were uncannily agile. His broad frame loomed over Willem, who twisted to evade him, but Bram's grip was iron-like, his strength impossible to match as he drove his prey quickly into submission.

"What are you doing?" Lode growled from his hiding place. But the men ignored him, focusing now solely on François and Willem, who fought back as best they could. Lode watched, frozen, as one of the dock workers dug through François› pocket, pulling out a few coins and a small knife, while the other tore Willem's cloak, looking for anything valuable.

Unable to contain himself any longer, Lode stepped forward and shouted, "Stop that! We're not here to rob them!"

Klaas and Bram, already disgruntled by his previous demands, turned to him with sneers. "If you wanted us to go easy, you should've paid more than a single stuiver, boy," one of them snarled, pocketing stolen coins. "We're taking what we're owed."

In that moment of distraction, François and Willem took their chance. Bruised and shaken, they broke free and took off down the street, disappearing into the darkness. Lode cursed under his breath as he watched them go, his plan crumbling around him. He was left alone in the alley with his accomplices, who looked at him contemptuously and blamed him for the miscarried scheme.

Just then, the sharp clink of metal on cobblestone reached his ears—steady, deliberate, and unmistakable. Two sentries rounded the corner, the iron-shod heels of their boots striking the ground with cold, rhythmic precision. Lanterns swung from iron loops at their belts, casting a flickering light across the narrow street and freeing their hands for any unexpected trouble. The polished metal toes of their boots caught the glow. Their faces hardened as they took in the scene, the taller of the two narrowing his eyes.

"What's going on here?" one of them barked, his voice as sharp as the sound of their boots.

Desperate to salvage what he could, Lode stood at the empty spot where François and Willem had fallen moments before, feigning a triumphant look. "I've captured the sodomites mentioned in the letter posted at the Belfry last night!" he exclaimed, gesturing toward the cobblestones as if François and Willem were still lying there. "They fled, but I can identify them!"

The sentries eyed him suspiciously as Klaas and Bram hovered anxiously nearby. One sentry stepped forward. "Who are these men? Looks like a bit more than just helping rid the town of miscreants."

"We're innocent bystanders," Bram said, raising his hands and looking directly at Lode. "We saw the lad here roughing them up and robbing them! If anyone's got something to answer for, it's him."

As the sentries closed in, Lode's protests grew frantic, his voice rising in pitch. He looked less like the hunter he'd imagined himself to be and more like the hunted, teeth bared in a final, futile snarl.

"Is that so?" One sentry asked, stepping closer to Lode. "You were trying to bring them in for arrest... by robbing them first?"

Lode stammered, feeling the walls close in on him. "N-No, that's not—these men, they were supposed to help me bring them to you! They misunderstood—I told them to restrain the accused, nothing more!"

But the sentries' patience had worn thin. "Enough," one of them commanded, his voice hard as iron. "We'll sort this out down at the guardhouse. You'll be coming with us, lad, along with your so-called helpers."

Lode's accomplices tried to protest, but the sentries had heard enough. With swift efficiency, they bound the men's wrists, Lode's protests growing weaker with each knot they tied. As they led him away, he realized with sickening clarity how drastically his plan had unraveled.

Lode saw François and Willem standing at a distance on Geauwwerkersstraat, just beyond The Bear's entrance, supporting each other in quiet solace. Freed but slightly bruised, they watched him with expressions of mingled shock and pity, their eyes a painful reminder of the trust he had shattered. Fortune had reversed its course, leaving Lode at the mercy of a justice he couldn't control, his secrets and ambitions collapsing under the weight of his scheming. Once again, Lode realized, as with all his past plans, he'd misstepped; he had failed to think his plan through to the end, leaving himself vulnerable to outcomes he had hoped to avoid.

As the sentries marched them down the cobblestone street, their lanterns casting flickering shadows that seemed to mock him, Lode's heart raced, and his palms grew clammy. His thoughts churned in desperation as he leaped ahead to salvage what little he could from the wreckage of his plan.

This isn't over, he told himself, biting back his panic. The guards will see the reason once I explain. I'll tell them about the letter, the accusations, and the danger François and Willem pose to Bruges. Indeed, they'll believe me and act. Once we're at the guardhouse, I'll ask the magistrate to issue a warrant for their arrest. A signed order will set things right.

His thoughts latched onto the idea like a lifeline, clinging to the hope that, even now, he could regain control. François and Willem won't get away—not after this.

But even as he tried to steady himself with that belief, a flicker of doubt gnawed at the edge of his resolve. The cold reality of his missteps pressed in around him, and the weight of what he had done—and what he had failed to do—settled heavily on his shoulders. He was vulnerable, his doubts threatening to overwhelm him.

The Arrest

Beneath the moon's cold, watchful ken,
Two friends were seized by callous men.
Through Bruges' streets, the whispers flew,
Of sins unproven, rumors grew.
The guards marched forth, the verdict grim,
Their freedom lost on justice's whim.
Yet side by side, they faced the night,
Their bond unbroken by the fight.

Bruised but upright, François and Willem began their cautious trek home, heading northeast along Vlamingstraat away from the lingering lamplight of Market Square. The two lived only a few houses apart, their families bound by years of friendship. Their shoulders brushed as they walked, and they leaned into each other for reassurance.

They whispered in low, hurried tones, their voices barely audible, swallowed by the heavy night air. Every so often, the faint creak of a shutter or the rustle of leaves made them flinch, their eyes darting to shadows pooling in doorways and alleys.

"Did you notice them waiting to ambush us?" Willem asked, his voice trembling.

François winced, lifting a hand to the fresh bruise on his cheek. A sharp pain flared beneath his fingertips, a reminder of how close they'd come to actual harm.

"I didn't even see them coming," he murmured, his voice tight and unsteady. "Just shadows—until they were on us." He hesitated, his breath catching. "Do you think it was his doing? Lode?"

Willem nodded, his face darkening. "I'd bet my last coin on it," he muttered. Lode was the only man they knew with the gall to send a pack of ruffians after them and the cowardice to hide behind a letter laced with lies. "What did he call us?" he murmured as though saying the word aloud might make its sting sharper and solidify the lie. "Sodomites." He shook his head, his gaze averted. "How does a man defend himself from such a thing?"

François glanced around them before answering, eyeing the empty street as if it, too, could be listening. "It's not just us," he whispered. "His letter names Henric van der Velde as well. If he hears about this..." He wondered how the Canon would react. He was a powerful man both in the church and in town. Would he get involved? How would he explain this to the church? Van der Velde had shown kindness to them and trusted them. If Lode's poisonous letter tainted that trust, it could ruin everything.

Willem hesitated, his steps slowing. "So, should we go to him? Tell him what happened. I just..." His voice broke, uncertainty giving way to dread. "François, I fear it. If the Church takes up this claim... Bruges is already so set on rooting out sin."

François paused, and his silence carried the weight of his thoughts. He finally spoke, his voice quiet but steady. "That's the risk. The Church." He hesitated, his mind flickering between trust and betrayal, his closeness to Henric van der Velde, and his fierce loyalty to Willem. "If van der Velde stands by us, we might be safe. But if he doesn't, if he thinks there's merit to it, or worse, that our friendship is a liability..." His voice dropped to a whisper, barely audible, "We could be finished. Cast out. Judged. And all for what? Some twisted game Lode's playing."

Willem swallowed, a nervous edge creeping into his voice. "It's one thing to face a couple of drunkards throwing punches," he said, his voice breaking slightly, "but if this reaches the Church..." He trailed off, casting a wary glance around them. "They won't listen to us. We'll be silenced before we're even heard. If van der Velde has to choose between his reputation and ours..."

"Then we're on our own." He met Willem's gaze, his mouth set in a grim line.

They walked on in silence, each locked in thought. Cold, heavy air pressed down on them as they trudged forward, the chill numbing their bruises.

They entered Burg Square, passing by the Basilica of the Holy Blood. "It feels... wrong," François said, glancing at the chapel. "Isn't faith supposed to be about love? Forgiveness?"

Willem's brow furrowed. "But this isn't that. It's about laws and judgment, nothing more, and we'll end up in Gallows Field."

François absorbed the weight of Willem's words. "That's the thing, though. The old laws are all about punishment, about rooting out what's seen as wrong and unclean. But the way I was taught—Christ's teachings—they're about mercy. Compassion."

"How did we get here, François? What do we do now?"

"We wait, Willem. I don't like it, but I'd rather face another street fight than risk the wrath of the Church—or worse, the town's courts with the Church behind them."

Willem gave a slow, reluctant nod. "We wait. And we tread carefully. Lode's letter is out there now, for all to see—beyond his circle of rats."

François glanced at Willem, offering a faint, weary smile. "Then we lean on each other, as we always have. We've made it through worse."

Yet, as the words left his lips, François couldn't shake the gnawing doubt. Had they truly faced anything as perilous as this? The weight of the Church's potential wrath loomed larger than any street fight they'd ever endured.

They continued down the darkened street, their shoulders touching as they steadied each other. They walked in the silence of unspoken fears.

Near the end of the street, purposeful footsteps grew loud behind them. Sensing the danger, François turned toward the sound, his eyes catching the faint flicker of light swaying with each step. Squinting into the unsteady glow, his steps faltered, and he gripped Willem's arm with a sudden urgency. The unmistakable silhouettes of city guards emerged, their lanterns casting shifting shadows that danced ominously across the cobblestones.

François turned to Willem, his eyes questioning. Why were the guards following them? Maybe it was about the earlier assault—to see if they were all right. But as the lead guard caught up to them, the tension in François' chest tightened.

"François van Daele and Willem de Clerck?"

They turned to face the guards. He knew then that this was not a courtesy encounter to inquire about their well-being. He stood tall and steadied his voice.

"Yes, that's us. Is something the matter?"

The guard's stoic eyes, cold and uncaring, offered no comfort. With deliberate precision, he unfurled a parchment marked with the magistrates' seal—a stark emblem of authority François knew he could not defy.

"You're under arrest by order of the magistrates of Bruges in connection with charges of sodomy," the guard said, his with practiced dispassion. "An accusation was received anonymously, but you have both been named."

François' vision blurred momentarily, his breath catching in his throat. This was Lode's doing. Willem's voice broke beside him, trembling with disbelief. "This is a mistake. There's no truth to it. We've done nothing—"

"Save your words for the magistrates," the guard snapped, cutting Willem off. "We have our orders."

With nothing more said, the guards pulled leather straps from their belts and bound François and Willem's wrists. The straps felt slick and oily, reeking faintly of sweat and something darker—remnants of countless others who had worn them before. Bound and helpless, the two men were herded through Bruges' narrow, twisting streets. The familiar buildings around them loomed like strangers, their windows watching the grim procession like nosy neighbors.

The guards marched them forward at a pace that left no room for hesitation. When François stumbled over a slick cobblestone, a rough hand yanked him upright, the grip biting into his arm. The pain shot through him, but he bit back any outward physical reflex or vocal utterance that would indicate his discomfort to the guard. François sensed delight in the guard's exercise of authority, and each step forward reminded him of his and Willem's fragility.

They felt the stares of townsfolk peering from windows behind slitted shutters, their faces ghostly in the pale moonlight. François kept his gaze forward, but the murmurs reached his ears nonetheless, sharp-edged whispers carrying rumors and accusations. Figures gathered in the shadows, some muttering, others braver. A harsh voice rang out, cruel and mocking: "Sinners!" Another jeered, "To the gallows with you!"

François' anger flared hot before he forced it down. He lifted his chin, determined to bear the shame with what dignity he could muster. But beside him, Willem faltered. The guard responded by tightening his grip on Willem's upper arm. He slowed, resisting the guard's hold to right himself and get back in step. Willem's voice raised in defiant protest. "This can't be happening! We've done nothing wrong!"

His words only drew a snort of disdain. The guard shoved him forward. "Save it for the judge."

As they passed The Bear, François' chest ached with an unexpected pang. He turned his head, half-expecting to see Lode lurking in the shadows, his sharp features alight with vindictive satisfaction. But the doorway was empty, offering no answers—only the bitter stillness of betrayal.

Willem looked to François, his expression a portrait of despair. His voice, when it came, was barely a whisper. "We were only trying to live as we were taught, to seek love and faith. How did it come to this?"

François met Willem's gaze, the weight of his words settling over him like a shroud. But he forced himself to speak, his voice low yet steady, a quiet strength threading through his sorrow. "Stay with me, Willem. They can judge us, condemn us…but they can't change who we are."

They turned their faces forward, their steps lagging against the brisk, practiced pace of the guards who led them. The streets of Bruges stretched ahead, foreboding and unfamiliar, and the uncertain fate that awaited them loomed heavy in the night. Yet, their solidarity remained unbroken, even as the shadows around them whispered of shame and fear.

Night Visitor

In Saint Jan's halls, where shadows crept,
Matthias lay whilst Bruges still slept.
A whispered curse, a blight to cleanse,
By fear and lies, the tale extends.
The Bear's kind voice, a cloak for pain,
Spoke truths of schemes both vile and plain.
The night grew thick with whispered dread,
As fate's dark path before him spread.

Matthias threaded his way back to Saint Jan's Hospital. Although he'd already spent one night there, the maze of alleys and passageways continued to disorient him, making it easy to lose his way. The detours gave him time to reflect on all that had transpired during his two days in Bruges. His thoughts circled back to François and Willem and the trouble they were facing—trouble stirred up by Lode.

Lost in thought, Matthias nearly stumbled past the familiar arched doorway, the sight of which grounded him back in the present. The hospital, a monument of history founded in the early 12th century, had grown over the centuries into an expansive facility, serving patients, pilgrims, and evolving medical practices.

He entered the infirmary hall, its high vaulted ceilings supported by wooden beams. He walked between rows of small beds lining both sides of the broad aisle to reclaim his place. The ward smelled of lifeless straw bedding mingled with the scent of herbal remedies. Now, at night, only candles and oil lamps provided illumination, creating a solemn and eerie atmosphere.

The sturdy wooden beds, raised on thick legs, starkly contrasted the simple pallets Matthias had slept on during his journey to Bruges. The narrow beds, thankfully lifted off the cold, dank floor, held coarse bedding: a thin mattress stuffed with straw and a rough wool coverlet for warmth. Matthias added his blanket from his travel bundle, spreading it over the hospital's standard fare. Privacy was minimal, with only thin curtains separating the beds, offering little distinction between the sick, the injured, or the healthy travelers. You never knew who might be sleeping beside you—perhaps ready to infect or rob you with little concern for your well-being.

Meanwhile, the nuns and monks—wearing simple habits and robes—acted as compassionate caregivers. Even at this hour, as Matthias settled into bed, a few crept around the hall, attending to the moaning sick with herbal remedies and prayer. As if performing a meditative ritual, like walking the Stations of the Cross, a solitary monk extinguished each oil lamp and all but one candle.

The faint scent of dried herbs permeated the air, no doubt carried from the hospital courtyard where medicinal plants were cultivated in tidy gardens. Matthias had noticed the apothecary's rows of thriving greenery earlier that day— an oasis of purpose amidst the somber infirmary. Those gardens, a testament to the hospital's commitment to healing, were a lifeline for patients with ailments ranging from fevers to wounds as the hospital worked to heal both the body and the soul.

But Matthias' healing felt far away. Sleep came upon him in fits and starts, each moment of rest interrupted by overwhelming worries for his new friends. François and Willem faced an uncertain future, and the rumors swirling through the gossip-laden town added to his unease. Why was Lode so bent on revenge? What could he do to help them?

He wanted to offer something—anything—but he was a stranger here, a journeyman with no prospects or connections to call upon for himself, let alone for the boys. As the night stretched on, sleep eluded him entirely, or if it came at all, he was unaware.

Until then, Matthias lay there listening to the muffled crunch of straw as those around him shifted in their beds. The murmurs of the nuns in prayer became indistinguishable from the soft groans and persistent coughs of those kept awake by illness. At one point, awake or in a dream lost between incantations for mercy and redemption, he thought he heard talk of breaking the curse on Bruges by purging the town of its unholy taint.

He noticed a faint rustling in the dead of night, the wolf's hour, as if someone stood near his bed. Opening his eyes, he saw a cloaked figure hovering quietly beside him. Slowly, the figure lifted a hand to her hood, loosening it and drawing it back just enough to reveal her face. The faint glow of the remaining candle caught her features, and Matthias recognized Margriet, the innkeeper's wife from The Bear.

"Matthias, I came to warn you about Lode," she whispered.

Matthias blinked, disoriented, the edges of sleep clinging to him like a dense fog. He pushed himself up on his elbows, wincing at the stiffness in his limbs. "Margriet?" he rasped, his voice thick with exhaustion. "What's Lode done now? What's happened?"

She leaned closer, her expression tense, as though every second wasted might cost them dearly. Her fingers brushed the edge of his cot as she glanced nervously toward the door.

"Lode's been whispering his poison all night," she hissed, glancing around as if the shadows themselves might overhear. "He's spun a web, and François and Willem are tangled in it. The warrant he persuaded the guards to issue—it's in play now. He's turned them over, raving about curses and unholy deeds. By morning, they'll be questioned before the magistrate."

She paused, her voice soft but edged with urgency. "Lode wears many faces, but behind each is the same hunger. He's failed in every honest trade, and now he's after something else—perhaps retribution or power he doesn't deserve. He spoke of purging Bruges of its blight."

Matthias blinked, the weight of her words sinking in. He pushed himself up on the straw-filled mattress, the coarse wool coverlet slipping to his lap. His voice, hoarse and barely above a whisper, broke the silence. "What do you mean? What blight?"

"There's still time, Matthias," she murmured, her eyes intense. "But tread carefully. Some men will do anything to rid this town of what they fear."

With that, she straightened, pulling her hood over her head and adjusting it to conceal her face. She vanished as quickly as she had appeared, and in her wake, she set an eddy of air in motion, causing the candle's flame to waver before sputtering out. The room fell into deep shadow, leaving Matthias in chilling solitude.

Sleep felt even more distant now. Matthias stared into the extinguished wick, where faint embers flickered in the darkness like dying fireflies. A wisp of smoke coiled upward, carrying the scent of burnt wax as the last sparks surrendered to the shadows.

Broken

In cells where light was thinly cast,
Two hearts endured, the hours amassed.
The magistrates with faces stern,
Decreed their fate where shadows churn.
"Confess thy sins," the gavel rang,
The air grew thick with judgment's pang.
Yet hand in hand, they bore the strain,
Though broken, love and faith remained.

Veiled gray light seeped through the high-barred window, barely enough to illuminate the cramped cell where François and Willem sat. The torchlight from the corridor had long since burnt out, leaving heavy shadows behind. The morning chill clung to the damp stone walls, and the air was thick with the mingled scents of mildew and unwashed bodies. Somewhere down the hall, a distant clatter broke the silence—guards stirring, the day beginning.

François sat slumped against the wall, his tunic damp from the moisture leeching from the stones. He stared at the uneven floor, his thoughts heavy and tangled. Every footstep or metallic jangle in the corridor tightened his stomach. The magistrates would summon them soon—he was sure of it. He glanced at Willem, hunched on the bench dejectedly. His friend had barely slept; François had heard his restless shifting through the long, cold hours of the night. Oddly, those sounds had kept him anchored, a reminder that he hadn't faced the darkness alone.

Willem stretched his stiff arms, clasping his hands tightly until his knuckles turned white. He gazed up at the tiny slit of a barred window high on the wall as if searching for something—a sign, perhaps, or a glimpse of the sky beyond the iron bars. He trembled as he tried to keep his composure, and his breathing came in shallow bursts. The fear from the previous night was still fresh in every movement.

François leaned back against the cold stone wall, his eyes drawn to the faint light seeping through the window. He blinked, unsure if exhaustion was playing tricks on him. A vast shadow swept across the sliver of light, briefly darkening the cell like a momentary eclipse. For an instant, a giant eye stared in—wide, unblinking, and all-seeing.

His breath caught, and he nudged Willem. "Did you see that?"

Willem looked at him, startled. "See what?"

François hedged, his gaze fixed on the now-empty window. "I thought…" He shook his head and forced a dry laugh. "Nothing. Just the light playing tricks."

Willem frowned but said nothing, his attention drifting back to the window above. Yet François couldn't shake the uneasy feeling that something—or someone—had been watching.

There was silence before Willem spoke, his voice barely audible. "I kept thinking…maybe someone would come. Maybe they'd realize it was a mistake." His voice cracked, the fragile hope he had clung to through the night slipping away. "But no one came, François. They won't."

François rested a steady hand on Willem's arm. "No one

will come to save us," he said, his tone low but firm. "But that doesn't mean we've lost. They don't decide who we are, Willem. We do."

Willem turned to him then, his pale face drawn with exhaustion. "How can you be so calm? They've already made up their minds. You know they have."

"I'm not calm," François admitted, his voice soft but firm. "I'm terrified. But we can't let that be all we feel. If they've already judged us, we hold on to what's true and what they can't take from us." He met Willem's gaze, his grip on his friend's arm tightening slightly. "And we face it together."

Willem's eyes shimmered, though he blinked quickly to keep the tears from falling. He let out a shuddering breath and nodded, though his movements were stiff and uncertain. "Together," he repeated as if testing the word, finding strength.

The guards' heavy and deliberate footsteps echoed down the hall. François straightened, his body taut with apprehension. They were coming closer, their shadows stretching ahead, reaching the pair before the guards themselves.

The guards grabbed them roughly, bound their hands again with leather straps, and marched them down the narrow corridor, their boots echoing sharply off the stone walls. François kept his head forward, his steps falling in time with the guards' measured pace.

His wrists chafed against the taut binding, but he ignored the sting. Beside him, Willem shuffled, his breath quickening with each step. François glanced sideways, catching the pale, haunted look in his friend's eyes.

"Steady," François whispered, his voice low enough that the guards wouldn't hear. "We'll get through this."

Willem nodded faintly but said nothing. The weight of his silence pressed heavily against François' chest.

The corridor led to a courtroom dominated by the magistrates' dais, an elevated bench carved from dark wood, polished, and engraved with the city crest. The magistrates sat high above, their high-backed chairs emphasizing their distant authority. Their faces were drawn and severe, and their robes stiff and dark.

A scribe, hunched over a desk, was deeply engrossed in his work to their right. Poised above a sheet of parchment, his quill trembled slightly. His beaky nose, mere inches from the page, seemed so close it was hard to tell if his nose, rather than the quill, was doing the work. Thick, untamed eyebrows jutted over his sunken eyes, giving his gaunt face a shadowy intensity. The scribe's bony fingers, spindly and exact, moved like the legs of a praying mantis—poised, purposeful, and methodical—as he dipped the quill into the inkpot. Scribbling furiously to keep pace with the unfolding scene, he seemed both predator and prey—his focus predatory, his jittering hands betraying a nervous vigilance as though he might dart away at the slightest provocation.

The courtroom clerk stood beside the scribe's desk, his slight frame bordering on emaciation. Their resemblance was undeniable: they had the same sharp features and skittish air, their shared tics and mannerisms like echoes of one another etched into their very being. They were twins.

But unlike the scribe, who wielded his quill like a natural appendage—a vital organ without which he would drop dead where he sat—his brother carried an authority borrowed from the scribe's meticulous wording, brandishing it like a weapon.

"François van Daele and Willem de Clerck," the clerk intoned, his reedy voice crackling like parchment being crumpled, each word jagged and uneven. "Step forward."

The guards prodded them forward until they stood in the center of the room, exposed under the magistrates' unrelenting gaze. François squared his shoulders, ignoring the icy knot forming in his stomach. He couldn't show weakness—not now, not here.

The magistrate to the left leaned forward, adjusting his spectacles as he unrolled a parchment. "You stand accused of committing the crime of sodomy," he said, his voice deliberate, the words slicing through the air. "A vile and unnatural act against the laws of this city and the will of God. How do you answer these charges?"

François felt Willem stiffen beside him, his breath catching audibly. François took a step closer, brushing against Willem's arm, and spoke before the silence could stretch. "We are innocent of these charges," he said, his voice steady despite his pounding heart. "There's no truth to them."

The magistrate raised an eyebrow, his expression unreadable. "An accusation has been made. Witnesses have named you both."

François narrowed his eyes. Witnesses? The word felt like a trap, baited to draw him into protest. "Who has named us?" he asked, his tone sharper than he intended. He thought of Lode's proclamation, but witnesses?

The central magistrate's gaze hardened. "The name of the accuser is irrelevant. The accusation stands. The truth will be uncovered through this court's methods."

François' pulse quickened, but he forced himself to remain

still. His jaw tightened. The name—singular. No mention of witnesses now, only Lode. "If there is truth to uncover," he said evenly, "then we will speak it."

The scribe's quill scratched against the parchment, recording every word. Willem's trembling had subsided, but François could feel his tension radiating like heat. He wanted to reach out, to reassure him, but the guards flanking them left no room for even the slightest movement.

The magistrate on the right leaned back in his chair, his lips curling into a faint, disdainful smirk. "Do you deny ever engaging in such acts? Are you prepared to swear your innocence under oath?"

François wavered. The question wasn't one of innocence but of survival. He knew what swearing falsely before the magistrates could mean—but the truth, spoken plainly, would seal their fate just as surely. He opened his mouth, but Willem's voice broke through before he could talk, cracking with desperation.

"We've done nothing wrong," Willem said, his voice rising. "We've lived as we were taught, as men of faith. This accusation is a lie!"

The three magistrates exchanged glances, expressions unreadable. The one seated in the middle raised his hand to silence the room. "Enough," he said. "You will have your chance to answer in full. You will return to your cell until you can be questioned more persuasively. After that, the veracity of your claims will be clear."

The guards stepped forward, their hands roughly clasping François and Willem's arms. François turned his head slightly, catching Willem's wide, panicked eyes. "It's all right,"

François murmured, his voice steady despite the storm churning within him. "We're still together."

Willem didn't respond, letting the guards guide him toward the door. François followed, his thoughts swirling like eddies in a stony stream. He had spoken the truth, but it felt like a drop of water against a stone wall. Whatever came next, it was clear the magistrates had already branded them guilty. The battle ahead would be for their freedom and their very humanity.

Veritas Dolorosa

Beneath the stones where shadows press,
Two souls endured in bleak distress.
A door loomed vast, its secrets steeped,
Through cracks, the blood of anguish seeped.
In restless dreams, Knowledge did rise,
A painted mask with piercing eyes.
"Speak thy truth," its whispers tolled,
"Face the night, and thou art bold."

The boys did not return to the holding cell where they had spent the night but were escorted by four guards, two in front and two behind, through a maze of winding hallways, seemingly endless and haphazardly constructed, as if on a whim rather than with careful planning. Eventually, they reached a long, sloping passageway, their feet slipping on the raked, wet stone until they stopped before a large wooden door.

One guard pulled a ring of keys from his belt and inserted a black iron key into the lock. The door howled as it swung open, revealing a vast, cavernous room. It appeared circular to François, like a cellar deep beneath a tower. A stone stairway, narrow and rail-less, spiraled down the moist wall like a scar. With a shove, the guards herded François and Willem toward the stairs and down to the floor below.

François stared at the surroundings. There were no beds, just straw on bare stone for sleeping. A bucket for human waste sat in one corner while iron rings on chains hung along the walls. When used, these restricted prisoners' movement, forcing them to stand or slump painfully to the floor. Leg restraints allowed only crawling to the waste bucket, no farther.

Benches arced along a section of the wall where half a dozen men sat, filthy and bleeding, their faces hollow with neglect and pain. François and Willem were separated, to François' dismay, and shackled in leg irons. They remained standing, trying to avoid the stares of their dungeon mates as the guards climbed the stairs and disappeared. The door slammed shut, cutting off the light, except for a solitary beam that entered through a narrow slit near the ceiling, perhaps meant for ventilation—the metallic slide of the bolt locking secured their fate.

François watched Willem from across the room; his chest tightened with worry. They'd been so close during their ordeal that he feared his friend would not survive without him nearby. François shifted his weight, the iron shackles biting into his ankles. His gaze wandered through the oppressive gloom like a blind man straining to hear a distant sound. The air reeked of damp stone, human filth, and something metallic—blood, long dried but never forgotten.

Then he saw it.

A massive door loomed on the far side of the room, barely visible in the faint beam of light. It absorbed the surrounding darkness, oppressive even in shadow. Thick oak planks, scarred and gouged as though by desperate hands, formed the bulk of the door. Stains mottled the wood—ambiguous in origin but unmistakably sinister. Diagonal iron straps reinforced it, their rusted surfaces exuding an air of unyielding strength.

François couldn't look away from the heavy iron ring that

served as the handle, tarnished and cold even from this distance. It beckoned—not with invitation, but with grim certainty. Above the frame, carved into the damp stone, were the words "Veritas Dolorosa." He squinted, his limited Latin teasing out the meaning: The Painful Truth. A knot twisted in his stomach. Was it a warning? A declaration? Or an omen?

François let his gaze drift downward, noting a dark stain pooling at the base of the door, seeping into the cracks of the stone floor. Whatever had leaked through had long since become one with the dungeon itself, a permanent marker of suffering. Despite the dank air, his throat went dry, and his imagination conjured the groan the door would make if opened—a mournful cry of resistance before revealing horrors no one should see.

He closed his eyes, but the image of the door remained, merging with other truths he could no longer suppress. He and Willem had been taken to van der Velde's chambers, their intimacy forced and painful. The Canon's cruelty humiliated them and abused them. The truth was unbearable, yet it clung to him like the damp chill of the dungeon.

François glanced toward Willem's still form. For Willem's sake, if not his own, he would face whatever lay beyond that door.

Sleep finally overtook him, restless and fragmented.

François stood unshackled in a vast expanse of mist. The air was still and cold, carrying faint, indistinct, and urgent whispers. From the fog emerged an immense figure: a giant puppet, skeletal and ethereal, its mask painted with haunting precision. It moved fluidly, its joints creaking softly as though guided by unseen strings.

François' breath caught. It was Knowledge. He recognized the puppet from the Procession of the Holy Blood, where it had loomed above the crowd in the morality play, serene but unyielding. When he first saw it, awe mingled with unease, a feeling that now returned, magnified by its ghostly manifestation.

The puppet's painted eyes were alive, piercing him with accusation and compassion. Its soft yet sharp voice resonated through the mist as though speaking directly into his mind.

"François, thou dost dream, but this is no illusion. I am Knowledge, summoned by thy troubled heart to speak what thou wouldst not."

François stepped back, his pulse quickening. "You're... from the procession. I saw you. Why are you here?"

The puppet tilted its head, its painted lips unmoving but its voice clear.

"Thou saw me, yet heeded me not. Now, amidst thy torment, thou hast called me forth. Thou knowest why I come."

François' voice trembled. "To mock me? To punish me?"

The puppet's skeletal hand rose, pointing toward him.

"Nay, not to mock, nor to punish, but to reveal. Thy silence is thy torment. Thy truth shall be thy strength. Speak what lies within thee. Claim what thou darest not. Face what thou canst not flee."

His eyes flew open. The dungeon remained unchanged, oppressive in its darkness. Yet, Knowledge's voice haunted him. The time for silence had passed. Soon, the moment would come when he would need to speak, claim, and face his love for Willem.

The Confession

In chambers dark, where torches bled,
A prisoner's truth in anguish said.
The iron turned, his spirit frayed,
Yet silence broke when hope betrayed.
A giant's voice, a dream's command,
"Thy truth must rise, though fear shall stand."
The priest's vile acts, the pain untold,
Revealed through tears, the silence cold.

The oaken door groaned on its iron hinges, a sound that scraped François' nerves raw as he was shoved into the chamber. The air here was heavier, clinging to his skin and carrying the sour tang of blood, excrement, and despair. The faint flicker of torchlight breathed life into the shadows of cruel implements hanging on the walls. François didn't need to understand their purpose to feel their threat; their presence alone suffocated him.

The iron chains now secured François' wrists and ankles as he shuffled forward, their weight a constant reminder of his captivity. The manacles bit into his skin with every movement, leaving raw marks that burned. Willem tried to keep step beside him, his chains rattling faintly. François reached out instinctively to offer him comfort, but the guards flanked the pair closer, knocking François' arms down. He had no choice but to focus on Willem's pale face, willing his friend to remain strong even as his courage faltered.

François felt Willem's presence like a lifeline, but fear gnawed at him. He knew the inquisitors wouldn't stop with him. They would break them both before the end.

The three interrogators waited, their robes black as shadows, their faces masked, their heads hooded, blending into the soot-darkened walls as if to ease their guilt. One of the men stepped forward, his voice calm, calculating, and laced with malice. "Take the big one," he commanded, gesturing toward François. "Let his little friend watch and learn how weak he is."

François' stomach sank as the guards dragged him to the center of the chamber. His chains scraped loudly against the stone floor, the sound of a mournful wail. Willem called out, but his cries were ignored. The guards forced François onto his knees before securing him to a tilted wooden frame reminiscent of a rack, leaving him vulnerable and exposed. His chains were momentarily removed, only to be threaded through iron rings at the top of the frame and refastened, stretching his arms high above his head. Iron cuffs replaced his ankle restraints, locking him in place.

The first instrument chosen was a small, cruel, and deceptively simple thumbscrew. One of the inquisitors held the device aloft, its dark metal glinting in the flickering torchlight. "A fitting start," he murmured as if discussing a mere formality. François' breath quickened as his hands were wrenched forward, and his fingers trembled as they were locked into the cold iron clamps of the device.

"Speak now," the inquisitor said sharply, "and save yourself the pain."

François clenched his jaw, fear warring with his

determination to hold on for as long as possible. The first turn of the thumbscrew sent a jolt of pain shooting through his hands, sharp and immediate. He gasped but refused to cry out, though his resolve began to fray.

Willem surged against his chains, his voice cracking with desperation. "Leave him alone! Please, stop!" His words echoed hollowly off the stone walls, falling into the same void as François' silent agony.

The inquisitor turned his head slightly toward Willem, his expression unreadable. "Ah, your friend is loyal," he mused. "But loyalty has no place here. Watch closely, boy, and learn the price of defiance."

Another turn of the screw, and François couldn't hold back his cry. The sound tore from his throat, raw and involuntary, as the sharp, relentless pressure sent waves of fiery pain radiating up his arms. His body trembled, his legs straining against the cuffs that held him bound to the frame. Each rasping inhale dragged the metallic stench of the room deeper into his lungs.

Willem's face crumpled, his horror stark and visible even in the dim haze of the dungeon. His voice cracked as he whispered, "François...just say something. Anything."

François' head sagged forward, his breath shuddering as tears stung his eyes and blurred the flickering torchlight. The thought of speaking, of giving the inquisitors the words they demanded, felt like a betrayal—not just of himself, but of Willem. The screws bit savagely with each turn, grinding against bone and resolve alike. The pain gnawed at his strength, stripping him bare, leaving him exposed, vulnerable, and hollowed out by the relentless force devouring him. The inquisitor knelt beside François, his voice low and insidious. "Do you feel that, boy? That is the truth trying to claw its way out. Set it free, and the pain will stop. Tell us of the Canon."

François shook his head weakly, his lips trembling. "I—I have nothing to say."

A sharp laugh escaped the inquisitor. "Then we will teach you how to speak."

Another turn. The wooden screws bit into the thin layer of skin covering his thumbs, the friction raw and unrelenting, as if the flesh itself were a failing buffer. François' scream tore through the chamber, jagged and piercing. The sound shattered something deep within Willem, who thrashed so violently against his chains that the guards had to wrestle him back into submission.

"Stop it! You're hurting him!" Willem shouted, his voice raw and desperate.

The inquisitor rose and fixed Willem with a cold, steady gaze. "No, boy. Not yet. He is stronger than he seems. But every man breaks. And when he does, so will you."

François' head drooped, his body trembling as the pain overwhelmed him. He blinked, his vision swimming. The torchlight dimmed, shadows deepening until they swallowed everything. Out of the encroaching void, a towering, skeletal figure emerged.

It was *Knowledge*. François recognized it immediately, though the memory felt distant, as though pulled from another life. The puppet's massive form filled the chamber, yet it felt insubstantial. Its wooden joints creaked softly as though moved by invisible strings. Its painted eyes glowed faintly, unblinking as they fixed on him.

The puppet's lips did not move, but its sharp, otherworldly voice resonated through the haze, piercing his mind.

"François, thou art bound not only by chains of iron but also of fear and silence. Thy truth festers within, burning deeper than these tortures. Wilt thou endure, only to deny it still?"

François' breath came in ragged gasps, his body trembling under the strain of the rack. "You don't understand," he whispered, his voice barely audible. "If I speak, I betray him and myself."

Knowledge tilted its head, its unyielding gaze piercing him.

"The Painful Truth is no betrayal—it is thy liberation. Thy silence chains thee to this torment, yet thou fearest freedom more. Wilt thou embrace thy truth, or let darkness consume thee?"

The inquisitor's voice cut through the hallucination, cold and distant. "Speak, boy, or we'll see how far you can stretch before you break."

François blinked, sweat and tears blurring his vision. But the puppet loomed larger now, its presence impossibly vast, pressing down on him like the weight of his guilt.

"The hour has come, François. Thy truth is thy only salvation."

François stirred at the command, the sight of Willem's terror-stricken face giving him the final push he needed. Knowledge's words resonated: *"Do not let thy fear break him."*

"Stop! Please!" François cried out in a hoarse voice, not knowing whether he was speaking to the puppet or the torturer. "I'll speak. I'll tell you what you want."

The inquisitor paused, raising a hand to halt the guards. He stepped closer, his expression cold and expectant. "Good. Then begin. Tell us of the priest."

François' gaze darted to Willem, whose wide eyes

brimmed with terror and pleading. François swallowed hard, tears streaking his face as he began.

"He...he met us at Saint Jan's Hospital," François stammered, his voice shaking. "He said he wanted to help us, to give us a safe place to stay. But then he started inviting us to his home."

The inquisitor tilted his head, his tone calm but insistent. "And what happened there?"

François faltered, his entire body trembling. "He made us do things. Together and separately." His voice cracked, and he closed his eyes, forcing himself to continue. "He liked to use a candle. First. Before he took us."

"A candle?" the inquisitor pressed, his tone sharp with curiosity. "Explain."

François nodded weakly, his words tumbling out in a broken stream. "He would use it to...to violate us first. Then he would take us. He did it until he was spent."

The inquisitor narrowed his eyes. "Describe 'spent.'"

François' face burned with shame, and his voice dropped to a whisper. "Until...wetness came out of him."

There was silence for a moment, the weight of François' words hanging heavy in the air. Then, the inquisitor gestured for him to continue.

François' voice cracked as he went on. "Sometimes he couldn't perform. He said he couldn't get firm like a bough. Not with us. Not with anyone. He said that even if he were with all the women in the world, it wouldn't matter."

The inquisitor turned to Willem, bound and trembling. "And you, boy. Is this true? Did the priest do these things?"

François' heart broke at the sight of Willem's pale face.

He could see the anguish in his friend's eyes, the humiliation of what they were being forced to admit. "Leave him alone!" François shouted, his voice raw. "You have what you want. I've told you everything. Stop!"

The Trial

To court they led the broken pair,
Where torches burned with flickering glare.
Confessions read, their truths laid bare,
Yet justice bowed to Church's care.
The priest untouched, his robes pristine,
His sins dismissed, his conscience clean.
For François and Willem, the lash was decreed,
While whispers of pity fell to greed.

On the third day of their confinement, guards retrieved François and Willem from the cold, damp cell. The shackles on their wrists and ankles bit into their skin as the guards led them through the narrow, torch-lit corridors of the courthouse, their boots echoing off the stone walls. Outside, the brisk morning air had offered a fleeting moment of clarity, but the courtroom swallowed it whole, replacing it with a suffocating, oppressive atmosphere.

The heavy oak doors creaked open, and all eyes turned to the accused. The guards halted just short of the magistrates' dais, forcing François and Willem to bow their heads beneath the weight of public scorn. Whispers wound through the assembled onlookers, their curiosity insatiable. Some craned their necks for a better view; others shielded their eyes or looked away, unwilling to meet the eyes of men so publicly disgraced.

A crudely constructed wooden pen stood at the center

of the courtroom floor, its splintered planks and rusted nails at odds with the grandeur of the magistrates' high-backed chairs. The guards locked François and Willem in the pen, its cramped space forcing them to stand shoulder to shoulder, their movements restricted by the iron bands around their limbs.

François looked at the guards, then at the gossiping crowd, and finally at the magistrates enthroned on an elevated bench. Their lofty position was an uncrossable chasm; the tableau was a reminder that justice was not impartial but distant, untouchable, and unmotivated.

The crowd settled when a thin, fidgety man with a reedy voice stepped forward, clutching a rolled parchment. The scroll contained a sanitized version of the alleged crimes, stripped of sordid particulars the court deemed too inflammatory or indecent for public airing. François clenched his fists, knowing that even without the whole truth, the court had already condemned him in their minds.

"François van Daele and Willem de Clerck," the clerk began, unrolling the parchment with a flourish. "You are hereby charged with grievous sins against nature, incitement of immoral acts, and conduct unbecoming citizens of Bruges. Let it be known that these accusations, brought forth by credible testimony and confirmed through inquiry, fall within the purview of this court's authority."

The crowd murmured as the charges were read, a current of suppressed excitement running through the room. François' stomach churned as he felt dozens of eyes on him, their judgment sharp, their minds already made up.

The clerk's voice droned on, reciting charges in stiff,

formal language, but François hardly heard them, his ears buzzing with the weight of his fear. By the time the clerk finished, his hand shaking slightly as he rolled the parchment back up, the courtroom had fallen silent.

The presiding magistrate busied himself signing off on court rulings, occasionally lifting his head to fix François or Willem with a practiced glare as if he were listening or even cared. It was less an expression of judgment than weariness, as though he had endured a hundred such cases and saw no novelty in this one.

When the clerk's recited litany arrived at the accusations against the priest, the magistrate's quill stopped twirling, annoyance passing over his face like a shadow. Tension rippled through the other magistrates, their collective discomfort betraying the political minefield of the accusation before the presiding magistrate silenced the crowd with a wave, signaling the clerk to step back.

"The court acknowledges these other accusations as well," the presiding magistrate began, "however, this court is not the arbiter of Church matters."

Standing to the side, the clerk glanced longingly toward the open window, where the faint sound of a bustling market carried on the breeze.

The finality of the magistrate's words was underscored by the silence that followed. François and Willem stood motionless. François had hoped the priest's crimes would be laid bare too, but the magistrate's words crushed that hope. How could the institution that preached morality and justice have become a fortress for the corrupt?

"We leave the judgment of his soul to God."

The magistrates exchanged approving glances at sidestepping a politically fraught accusation.

Willem's voice shattered the stillness, hoarse and raw with anger. "It isn't right! He—"

"Silence!" barked one of the guards, punctuating his command with a heavy-handed blow. Willem staggered, his chains rattling as he stumbled, but the cramped confines of the pen allowed no space for him to fall, leaving him teetering but upright, his eyes blazing with defiance.

"Control the prisoner," the magistrate said coldly, his voice carrying the weight of authority. "We will not have this court reduced to chaos."

François felt Willem's fury radiate off him like heat, but he fixed his gaze on the floor. It was easier not to look at the magistrates, to avoid seeing the disdain—or worse, the disinterest—in their eyes. He knew their minds were already elsewhere: on the feast awaiting them at home, the lingering smell of the gallows where they'd soon send him and Willem, or the cases file in their stacks.

When the sentence was pronounced, it came with a practiced flourish, as though the presiding magistrate were reciting lines from a play. "By order of this court, François van Daele and Willem de Clerck, found guilty of grievous sins against nature, shall face public punishment at Gallows Field—flogging and burning their hair—and are hereby exiled from Bruges."

The magistrates rose from their seats before the final words were spoken. Their robes billowed as they moved toward the exit, their departure swift and businesslike. Sensing his dismissal, the clerk gathered his papers and followed.

François and Willem were left standing in their shackles, the echo of their chains the only sound in the suddenly vacated room.

To François, the court's indifference was a punishment in itself. The magistrates' vacant gazes and hurried retreat spoke a silent verdict. Justice, it seemed, was not blind—it simply chose to look the other way, leaving the priest's sins untouched and the weight of accountability to crush those least able to bear it.

He scanned the courtroom, the silence amplifying the whispers and murmurs that bubbled up from the crowd. His eyes landed on the back of the room, where his mother sat stiffly beside his father. Willem's parents were beside them, equally rigid, as though their shame had turned them to stone. His mother's face was pale as alabaster, her hands trembling as they clutched a handkerchief. She looked small, shrunken, like a ghost of herself.

François knew she had wanted to stay away—oh, how she must have wanted to avoid the stares and whispers of the crowd—but the bond of a mother to her child had dragged her here, no matter the cost. When the magistrate delivered the verdict, François saw his father flinch as though struck in the chest. His mother reached for his hand, but he pulled away, his face a mask of stone, his body rigid with some unknowable agony.

"Don't let them see," his father muttered, his voice barely audible over the murmurs.

François' stomach churned. Was it shame in his father's voice? Grief? His mother sat frozen, the handkerchief pressed to her lips. François could only guess at the storm raging inside her. Did she mourn her son, or did she mourn the life they had lived before the trial? Was she ashamed of him or too tired to fight the shame clawing at her insides?

As the crowd hissed and murmured, their verdict echoing the magistrate's words, François couldn't look at her anymore. He couldn't bear to see her shame—or worse, her sorrow. He looked to Willem, whose head was bowed, and then to the wooden floor beneath his feet, wishing it would open and swallow him whole.

Sanctuary

In gilded halls where shadows creep,
The judges feast while secrets seep.
A crucifix with firelight's grace
Mocks piety upon his face.
Wine and whispers dull the guilt,
While mercy's plea in darkness wilts.
To wealth and power, oaths are sworn,
As cries of truth die, unmourned.

Though plump, Canon Henric van der Velde seemed diminished as he sank into an ornately carved chair upholstered in rich burgundy velvet. The goblet in his hand, its stem crafted of gleaming silver and brimming with ruby-red Spanish wine, reflected the hearth's firelight and wickfire from honey-scented beeswax candles.

His apartment was cloaked in lush embroidered tapestries and religious icons set in bejeweled frames worthy of a cathedral's altar. Despite the room's opulence and religious iconography, it felt more cluttered than sacred, devoid of true sanctity or piety. A long oak table at the center of the room groaned under the weight of roasted capons, fresh-baked bread, and imported fruits from the south. The sweet aroma of the food mingling with the heady tang of frankincense, created a sensory symphony that blurred the line between devotion and excess. He ate alone.

Henric gazed at the silver crucifix above the mantel,

its serene Christ glowing in the firelight. Sanctuary was not just a refuge but a thing of beauty, he thought—a refuge for the righteous, a shield against the world's chaos. But like all shields, it protected only those who wielded it.

Brother Anselm, his trusted intermediary, had attended the proceedings on his behalf earlier in the day and reported that the trial had been swift. The boys had confessed. Their sins would be absolved tomorrow amid lash strokes and burning pyres, rising as smoke to the heavens.

A treatise on morality, its spine broken from centuries of use, lay on the table beside him. He picked it up and thumbed through pages brittle from age. He stopped to read a passage aloud: "Justice, tempered by compassion, reveals the true heart of the faithful."

The idealistic words grated against his practical mind. They stirred thoughts he preferred to keep buried, emotions he had long since dismissed as useless, a burden he refused to carry.

"Compassion," he muttered, his voice laced with scorn, "is a luxury for those who can afford it." With disdain, he set the book aside, its wisdom too distant, too naïve and impractical for the world he knew.

He stretched, his silk robe rustling as he reached for a dish of sugared almonds. Outside, a muffled bell tolled the hour. His thoughts flickered briefly to the events of the day— the trial, the accusations, the faint possibility of an inquiry beneath the basilica, should the collegium care enough to peer beyond their ceremonial veils. He reasoned that François and Willem's suffering was the natural price of their sins, not his burden to bear. When he had a moment, he would inscribe their names onto his intercessory prayer roster—a small mercy, he supposed—and intercede for their souls in due time. The list was long, and he was a busy man. Whether such prayers made a difference was a question he neither knew the answer to nor cared to dwell upon.

A sharp knock interrupted Henric's musings. Frowning, he gestured irritably for Brother Anselm to answer the door.

The heavy door creaked open, revealing Lode standing hunched on the threshold, his face pale and drawn. His clothes were rumpled, his hair slick with sweat. Anselm hesitated, but Henric waved him off dismissively.

"Let him in," Henric said, his tone laced with irritation.

Lode shuffled into the room, his disheveled image mirrored in the polished silver frames and jeweled icons encircling him as though reflected in a thousand accusing eyes. "My lord," he began, his voice trembling, "I came to seek your counsel."

Henric leaned back in his chair, steepling his fingers. "My counsel? I recall offering it before, Lode, only for you to overstep your bounds. Why do you return now?"

Lode swallowed hard, his Adam's apple bobbing in his throat. "I made a mistake, my lord. I thought...I thought we shared something more. I was wrong. But I didn't mean to offend you."

Henric's expression hardened, the faintest sneer curling his lips. "Offend? No, Lode. You presumed. And in presumption lies the root of many sins."

"I—I understand," Lode stammered. "But I thought you'd want to know... the boys confessed."

Henric raised an eyebrow, feigning indifference. "And

why should that trouble me? Their confessions, whatever they may be, are of no consequence to me. The Church's sanctity remains intact, as does mine."

"But...but you were also mentioned," Lode pressed, his voice rising with desperation. "What if they—"

"Enough." Henric rose abruptly, his robe billowing around him like a mantle of authority. "Lode, your insinuations tire me. Whatever they've said or however I've been implicated, the Church will protect its own. Do you doubt that?"

"No, my lord," he mumbled.

"Very well then, let this be the last time you come to me." Henric gestured toward the door. "Leave."

Lode hesitated, desperation bubbling to the surface. "You can't just dismiss me like this," he blurted. "I've done everything for you! I've been loyal," he stammered, his voice cracking.

Henric turned, his gaze cold and unyielding. "Loyalty? To whom? To me, or your ambition? Do not mistake your schemes for faithfulness, Lode."

Lode's mouth trembled as he whispered, "I could tell everyone what I know."

Henric stepped closer, his eyes narrowing. "And what, pray, do you know that wouldn't damn you tenfold before it scratches me?" His faint smile sharpened. "Go ahead, Lode. Speak your truth. Let's see who they burn first."

Lode's defiance crumbled. His shoulders sagged, and he turned toward the door. It slammed shut behind him, leaving Henric alone once more.

Henric stared at the closed door, a flicker of unease clouding his thoughts. From the dungeon in nearby Burg Square, muffled cries clawed through the barred windows, rising into the chilled night air like ghostly pleas destined never to be heard. Unfazed, he called for more wine. Anselm hurried to fulfill the request. Henric eased back into his chair, his goblet refilled. His gaze moved from the glowing crucifix to the licking flames below, his ears deaf to the cries outside, his mind resolute against the stirrings of conscience.

Warning

In The Bear's warm glow, fear did stir,
As whispers rose, soft and unsure.
"The boys are doomed," Matthias cried,
"Their fate unjust, though laws abide."
Margriet wept, her voice was dire,
"Beware of Lode, his heart's on fire.
He twists the truth, a wolf in wait,
To bind thee too in François' fate."

Outside the town hall, the crier's voice rang out every hour, loud and unfeeling, reporting the news: "By order of the magistrates, François van Daele and Willem de Clerck, found guilty of grievous sins against nature, shall face public punishment at Gallows Field—flogging and the burning of their hair—and are hereby exiled from Bruges."

Matthias watched from the edge of the crowd, dread coiling in his stomach as the crier's voice rang out, hammering the sentence into the restless throng. He spotted Lode, a familiar figure, leaning against a post, his lips twisted in a smug smirk as he observed the crowd. A shiver ran through Matthias, not from the cold but from the memory of Lode's venomous threats the night he had turned the magistrates' eyes toward François and Willem. He knew Lode had orchestrated this and had spread his poison until it reached the ears of those in power. Matthias felt utterly powerless, a mere spectator as his friends were swept toward humiliation and pain, their fates sealed by forces beyond his control—and by the malice of one boy determined to destroy them all.

"They're just boys," Matthias muttered, but the rising din swallowed his words. Around him, the townsfolk buzzed with sordid interest, the punishment already a spectacle in their minds. Matthias clenched his fists at his sides, his mind scrambling for any way to intervene. But what could he do? He was a journeyman, a stranger in this town, with no standing or allies. He felt the weight of his impotence as heavily as François and Willem must have felt their chains.

The wind picked up, sharp and briny as it tore through the square, and Matthias turned his face away from the crowd, unable to bear the venom in their eyes. The punishment was set for tomorrow at Gallows Field, and the pyres were already being prepared. Every fiber of his being screamed to act, to stop this, but the walls around Bruges felt as impenetrable as the forces that had condemned his friends.

"I need to think," he told himself as the north wind tugged at him, its erratic gusts herding him toward The Bear. A dozen plans swirled in his mind, each dissolving as quickly as it formed. Could he bribe a guard? He had no money. Break them out before dawn? He couldn't do it alone. The parasitic cold clung to him like a second skin as wind bursts pushed and prodded him through the winding streets. What if the only thing he managed to do was get himself killed? The thought tightened its grip on him, his desperation threatening to swallow him whole.

The relentless wind delivered him to The Bear. Once inside, the innkeeper, Pieter, raised a hand in greeting, but his expression soon changed as he read Matthias's concern. He beckoned Matthias toward the scullery, where Margriet, her hands moving methodically, was busy scrubbing kettles, a routine aimed at distraction.

Matthias slipped into the shadowed room next to the kitchen to join the couple.

"They've sentenced them," Matthias yelled, his voice raw and trembling. "Tomorrow—at Gallows Field. Flogging, hair burning...exile."

The words hung in the air like a death knell. Margriet gasped, her hands flying to her apron. "Dear God, no. Not those boys. They don't deserve this..."

"They're going to parade them like criminals," Matthias continued, pacing the small space. "Humiliate them in front of everyone and cast them out like they're less than human. It's not justice—it's cruelty."

Margriet's voice was barely a whisper. "Those poor lads. What could they have done to deserve such punishment? It's not their fault—it never was."

Pieter leaned heavily on the counter, his frown deepening. "You've got a good heart, lad, but you can do nothing for them now. The magistrates have spoken. You stick your neck out any further for François and Willem, and you'll be next in line to face their wrath. It'd be a shame if you were to lose that beautiful hair to the irons or endure something worse."

"I can't just sit here and do nothing. They're my friends."

Margriet gently touched his arm, eyes glistening. "Sometimes, all you can do is pray. Pray, and keep yourself safe. They wouldn't want you risking your life for theirs.

Margriet glanced toward the door, lowering her voice. "There's another thing, Matthias. That boy—Lode. He's trouble."

Matthias' breath hitched. "I know that. He's the one behind all of this."

She wrung her hands, her voice trembling with urgency. "He hasn't forgotten what happened that night—how his first attempt to have the boys arrested went so wrong. Somehow, he blames you for the botched plan that landed him in jail, even if it was just for an hour. I've seen how he watches you—like a wolf on the roadside, waiting to pounce. And now, with François and Willem set to be punished, he'll feel justified in going after you."

Pieter cut her off, his tone firm. "It doesn't matter whether you're new in town or just met François and Willem; he's marked you. That lad's got a way of twisting gossip into a noose. Keep your distance, Matthias, or he'll drag you under along with the others."

The wind rattled against the scullery door as though announcing a new customer. A shout rang out from the tavern, piercing the stillness of the kitchen and seeping into the scullery. Matthias stiffened, his focus snapping to the sound. He knew that voice—Lode. It was unmistakable, sharp, and taunting even when muffled by thick wooden walls. A prickle of unease ran down his spine as Pieter's eyes flicked warily toward the door. Lode was back and in the main room, spreading his presence like a cold draft.

Margriet gripped Matthias' sleeve. "Watch yourself. That boy's sharp—always in the shadows, always listening for something to use."

"Stay back here for a few minutes, Matthias. Let him think you're not here." He reached for the door but paused, his hand hovering just above the handle. "And don't give him anything he can use against you."

Matthias nodded. He could feel Lode's presence even without seeing him.

Pieter and Margriet stalled at the scullery door after Matthias had fallen silent, exchanging weary glances. Margriet lowered her voice, her words barely a whisper, but Matthias could still make them out as she spoke. "We've given that boy too many chances, Pieter. I thought we were doing the right thing, but look where it's gotten us."

Pieter exhaled sharply, rubbing his temples. "You don't have to tell me, Margriet. I know. But we couldn't throw him out—what would've happened to him then? He was just a scrappy and wild boy when he showed up here. We thought a bit of structure would...straighten him out."

Margriet shook her head, her voice trembling. "He's not a boy anymore, Pieter. He's dangerous. He's dragging this place—dragging us—down with him. And now he's got Matthias tangled up in his mess. You heard what Matthias said. François and Willem—those boys don't deserve what's happening to them."

Pieter's tone hardened. "I know they don't. But tossing Lode out now won't fix that, will it? He's got a taste for power, and you know he'd find another way to stir up trouble—even if he's not under our roof."

Margriet wrung her hands. "So what do we do? Keep him here? Watch as he poisons everyone around him?" She glanced toward the kitchen door as though expecting Lode to be listening on the other side. "He's already hurt so many. What's next, Pieter? How far will he go?"

"I don't know. But I'll be damned if I let him drag this place under. Not after everything we've built."

Margriet nodded reluctantly, her expression grim. She touched Pieter's arm briefly before they pushed the door open and stepped into the main room. Their voices faded into the tavern's low hum, leaving Matthias alone in the scullery. Even the people who had shown Lode the most kindness and patience could barely defend him anymore.

Margriet's words returned to him, soft but firm: Sometimes, all you can do is pray.

Matthias stepped back into the main room, his heart heavy. His eyes darted to Lode, who stood behind the bar, his movements slow and calculated. Lode froze when he noticed Matthias approaching. Their eyes met, and Lode's lips curled into a malicious, smug smirk.

"Goodnight, Matthias," Lode said, his voice syrupy and mocking.

Matthias swallowed hard. He pulled the inn's door open only to find the wind waiting for him, briny and cold, curling around him like a predator testing the edges of his resolve. Ducking into the darkness, he set off toward Saint Jan's Hospital, the punishment of his friends gnawing at his thoughts.

Punishment

To Gallows Field the wagon creaked,
Where cries of wrath and scorn were wreaked.
Bare flesh exposed, the lash did bite,
And blood baptized the cruel daylight.
With hair alight in searing flame,
The branded bore their marks of shame.
Yet in their pain, a truth did glow:
Through fire, a strength began to grow.

The dungeon reeked of sweat, decay, and despair. François barely registered the clanging of keys until the door to their cell groaned open. A guard stepped in, his shadow spilling across the cold stone floor. "Van Daele. De Clerck. It's time to face your judgment."

François exchanged a glance with Willem, whose pallor betrayed his terror. Neither spoke. There was nothing left to say. They were roughly pulled to their feet, manacled, and led into the blinding light of the courtyard.

The procession awaited them—a convoy of creaking wooden wagons flanked by grim-faced guards, with the scaffold of justice rising stark against the gray horizon beyond the city gates. François' stomach churned as he noticed the other prisoners loaded onto similar wagons: men and women with bowed heads and boys no older than fourteen—Willem's age—trembling as they clutched their rosaries. Some bore the noose already around their necks; others wore heavy iron collars etched with the markings of their crimes. Each wagon groaned under its load, the sound mingling with the muffled sobs and distant jeers of the townsfolk lining the streets. A few, like François and Willem, were destined for the lash and the branding iron. Still, others, silent and resigned, were marked for the stake.

François and Willem were forced into their wagon, the rough planks biting into their knees as they knelt. The wheels groaned, and the parade began. Townsfolk lined the streets, their expressions ranging from pity to disgust. Some muttered prayers, others shouted insults. Children ran alongside the wagons, snapping at the wheels and jeering, while peddlers hawked roasted nuts and sweetmeats as though this were a festival. Others waved crude pamphlets in the air, recounting the crimes and sentences of the condemned in lurid detail. The mingling of commerce and spectacle made François' stomach churn; a cruel mockery of his suffering had become a marketplace distraction.

The wagon lurched forward, its iron wheels groaning against the uneven cobblestones of Philipstockstraat. The procession weaved through the heart of Bruges past the curious stares of the townsfolk lining Katelijnestraat, their faces marked by pity and disdain.

Children weaved deftly through the crowd and wagons. Their laughter echoed against the stone walls as they played a chasing game. One boy, arms outstretched, raced after his friends, his breath puffing in the chilly morning air. The others squealed as they dodged and ducked through the crowd with the carefree abandon only youth could claim.

As the wagon rattled past, one of the children suddenly

stopped. A boy stood frozen among the spectators, his wide eyes locking onto François' battered form. François held his gaze momentarily, seeing neither pity nor disdain—only raw and unfiltered fear. Then the boy was gone, swallowed by the shifting crowd.

As they approached Gentpoort, the massive stone arch loomed like the gaping maw of a beast, flanked by imposing towers that stood sentinel over the road; beyond, the Gallows Field waited, the rising smoke from its stakes a grim prelude to their fate.

François' eyes fell on the raised platform where the giant puppets from the recent play still stood. Knowledge appeared impossibly large among the grotesque figures, its hollow eyes locking with François'. The colossal figure moved as if unshackled from its strings, stepping off the platform and into the street. The crowd was oblivious, their voices and movements undisturbed. Only François could see it.

The puppet's wooden mouth opened, and though no sound came, François heard its words as clearly as if they were whispered into his ear.

"In thy most need, I go by thy side. Your reckoning draws near, François van Daele."

François' breath caught. He turned to Willem, but his friend stared ahead, his face a mask of dread. Knowledge stepped closer, its carved hand pointing toward the distant Gallows Field, where acrid smoke curled steadily into the sky.

"Look upon them," Knowledge intoned, nodding toward the other condemned men and boys. "Their fates, though harsh, reflect the reckoning of a world where compassion falters. Do you see their suffering as you see your own?"

François' gaze swept over the line of prisoners' wagons. One boy near him, perhaps no older than thirteen, sobbed openly as a guard struck him with the blunt end of a pike. In another wagon, a man slumped against the side bore fresh welts on his back, his shirt torn to reveal flesh raw and bleeding. Farther ahead, a woman, gagged and bound, stared vacantly toward the heavens, her face streaked with soot and tears. His stomach twisted at their suffering, a bitter reflection of his own.

"Mercy is the measure of a soul, François," Knowledge whispered. *"For what you give—even in thought—may yet be returned."*

The wagon jolted, and Knowledge vanished as suddenly as it had appeared. The world crashed back into focus: the shouts, the jeers, the grating rattle of iron wheels on cobblestones.

The pungent stench of charred flesh mingled with the sharp, coppery tang of blood as the caravan passed through the gates, revealing the Gallows Field. Stakes lined the perimeter, jutting skyward like skeletal fingers clawing at the heavens as if to reach God Himself. Some were already aflame, their victims charred and slumped, while a few had been reduced to smoldering embers, the ropes that bound them burned away.

Rough hands yanked François from the wagon and forced him to his knees. Before him sprawled the Gallows Field, an unholy tableau torn from nightmares. Stakes, smoke, and the twisted forms of the condemned converged in an End Times vision—flesh burned, souls writhed, and the living gorged on suffering.

The pale and hollow-eyed crowd seemed more like specters than the living, as though trapped in an eternal cycle of judgment and damnation. François felt ensnared, a sinner condemned to his place in this macabre feast, where the world devoured itself piece by piece.

Bloodlust hung in the air, a primal hunger that stripped merchants of their civility, turned neighbors into accusers, and transformed the pious into feral creatures reveling in the carnage. Guttural roars drowned the murmurs of prayer and lamentation as the crowd, no longer content to merely witness, hungered to be consumed by the spectacle.

The executioners wasted no time. François and Willem were stripped to the waist, placed in the stocks, their faces exposed to the waiting crowd, their backs bared to the hooded executioners standing over them. The executioners each held a scourge with several leather tails embedded with bone shards and hooks. The first strike tore through François' flesh, a searing line of pain that left him gasping. Willem cried out beside him, cutting through the crowd's clatter. François shut his eyes, trying to block out the sound, but each lash felt like it struck them both. The feral mob bayed, reveling in the brutality.

When the flogging ended, François' body spasmed, his back laced with parallel finger-length gashes that resembled chasms rimmed in strata of shredded skin wet with blood. Ragged gasps erupted from his lungs, each breath feeling like his last. He convulsed and spat in unproductive attempts to rid himself of the unendurable mental and physical anguish while the crowd cheered in satisfaction.

The executioners returned to the stage. Each carried an iron poker drawn from the brazier precariously perched at the edge of the stage. The faint hiss of burning embers mingled with the biting scent of scorched metal, reaching even the farthest corners of the silent, transfixed crowd. The rods glowed with a molten orange-red intensity, the air around them shimmering with heat. The stage creaked in protest under the weight of the brazier and rods and the dark purpose they carried as if recoiling from the grim spectacle about to unfold. An eerie light illuminated the gallows, transforming it into a macabre theater. The crowd murmured in anticipation.

The executioners waved them before the stocks, their heat rippling waves so that François, Willem, and the audience understood the promise of what would come. The audience cried a chaotic symphony of thrill and bloodlust. François' stomach churned.

Then came the first touch. A sharp hiss erupted as the iron met François' hair, the sound slicing through the din like a blade. He flinched, every nerve alight, his body instinctively recoiling against the restraints. The acrid stench of burning flesh and singed hair filled the air, thick and unrelenting, clawing at his throat. He gagged, bile rising as the vile scent seeped into his skin.

Pain radiated from the crown of his head down to his chest. His vision blurred, his mind teetering on the edge of delirium. He could barely hear the jeering crowd over the roaring in his ears, his thoughts fragmenting into incoherent shards: prayers, curses, pleas for mercy. The iron returned for another touch, and he screamed, the sound raw, primal, coming from the depths of his soul.

Time stretched into an eternity of torment. François fought against the rising haze in his mind, clinging to the fragments of himself not yet consumed by the agony. The heat, the stench, the relentless jeers—they blurred into a single, suffocating force, drowning him.

And yet, somewhere deep within, a spark of defiance remained—a fragile ember that refused to be extinguished, even as the molten iron hovered near again. When the ordeal concluded, remnants of scorched hair writhed around him, still smoking like a lit fuse. François slumped to the ground, his vision swimming. Beside him, Willem lay motionless, his quiet sobs almost drowned out by the crowd's clatter. Then, Knowledge reappeared, this time smaller, its form kneeling beside him.

"Your penance begins, but the journey is long," it said. *"Find in this suffering the seed of humility, for only through it may you sow redemption."*

The puppet's words echoed through his weakened consciousness, and in the depths of his pain, he began to sense the faint and fragile seed of redemption stirring.

Redemption

Through gallows' flame and lashing sting,
They fled where hopes in silence cling.
The spires of Bruges, now faint and small,
Gave way to fields where swallows call.
"Why must men hate?" François decried,
"When beauty blooms on every side?"
"Fear is their refuge," Willem did say,
"But love's the path we seek this day."

François plodded alongside Willem, each step pulling them further from the city they called home. Their backs ached from the lashes, their heads were bare and raw from the hot irons, and their souls were stripped of loving families and friends. Bruges lay behind them, its spires and canals shrinking away with each weary step.

The last light of the day gilded the fields with a soft, golden glow as barn swallows swooped and darted, their graceful movements untouched by the cruelty that had unfolded on Gallows Field. François glanced up, and for a fleeting moment, their flight carried a quiet promise—of hope, renewal, and safe passage.

"How is it," he began, breaking the heavy silence, "that the same people who cheer for punishment and cruelty can live surrounded by so much beauty? They can admire the work of human hands—the carvings on a church, the songs of a minstrel—and still turn on their fellow man with such ease?"

Willem glanced at him, his face lined with exhaustion but his expression thoughtful. "Perhaps it is easier to hate than to understand," he said. "Easier to follow the crowd than to ask questions."

François nodded but wasn't satisfied. The mob that had screamed for their pain, the magistrates who had twisted their words into confessions, the priests who had declared their punishment as divine justice—none of them had been personally wronged. And yet they had watched, some even smiling, as the whip tore into flesh and the flames singed their hair.

He shook his head, his voice trembling. "But why? Why are people eager to hurt someone who's done nothing to them?" François shook his head, his voice low. "It wasn't about justice. It was about putting on a show—about fear and feeling righteous at someone else's expense."

Willem said nothing, but his silence invited François to continue.

"How can the same hands that build cathedrals hold a whip so easily?" François whispered. "How can someone admire a sunset one moment, then turn away from another's pain?"

They walked silently, the gravel crunching beneath their worn boots. Darkness began to settle over the fields, yet the sky above remained streaked with hues of orange and pink as if refusing to surrender to the night. François' thoughts churned. Perhaps, he mused, humanity was torn between two forces: one that yearned for connection and harmony and another driven by fear and survival. Love and hate were not opposites but two sides of the same coin—born from the same deep well of emotion.

"Even after everything," François murmured, "there's still beauty in the world."

"And yet," Willem added quietly, "we're quick to destroy it—each other, the beauty we've built. Maybe it's because we're afraid of losing it...or because it shows us what we're not."

François frowned. "But why must fear win so easily? Why does it speak louder than love?"

Willem sighed. "Fear's simple—it asks for nothing. Love? That takes courage. You have to give, to trust...and risk being wrong." He sighed, his words far more significant than his fourteen years. "And not everyone is strong enough for that."

François looked at his friend, seeing a quiet wisdom he hadn't fully appreciated. The sun had nearly set, and the first stars were beginning to prick the sky. He thought about the kindnesses they had seen, small though they were: the innkeeper's extra bread, Matthias' loyalty, even the silence of some townsfolk who hadn't joined the mob. Those moments were like the stars breaking through the darkness.

"Maybe that's the answer," François said at last, his voice steadier now. "To hold onto love, even when fear surrounds us. To see the beauty, even amid pain. Maybe it's not about understanding why people are the way they are, but choosing to be different."

Willem smiled faintly, a rare and fleeting thing these days. "Then we have to be stronger than fear."

François nodded, his steps feeling lighter despite the ache in his body. The road ahead was long, and their future uncertain, but he felt a spark of hope as they walked beneath the darkening sky. Humanity was flawed, but so was he, and if he could find a way to keep love alive in his own heart, then perhaps others could, too.

The sound of hurried footsteps, faint at first but growing louder, broke the quiet. Willem tensed, his hand instinctively ghosting over his side, where once he might have carried a knife. François glanced back, his brow furrowing, but his expression softened when he recognized the figure sprinting toward them.

"Matthias?" he called, incredulous.

The journeyman skidded to a halt, bent over with his hands on his knees as he caught his breath. His belongings were bundled neatly in his leather pack slung haphazardly over one shoulder, and his face was flushed from the effort of running. "Wait!" he gasped. "You didn't think I'd just let you leave me behind, did you?"

Willem frowned. "Matthias, what are you doing? This road isn't meant for you."

"Neither is Bruges," Matthias replied, straightening. His tone was firm, though his voice trembled slightly. "I can bear no more of that place. Enough of the rumors, the fear, and how people tear each other down to feel righteous. It's no home of mine."

François' throat tightened. After everything they'd endured, the idea that someone would willingly follow them and share their fate felt almost too much to hope for. "Matthias, it won't be easy. We don't even know where we're going."

"I know enough," Matthias said, his voice unwavering. "South, you said? Toward a town where people are kinder and don't do not devour one another with suspicion. I would sooner have that than stay in a place rotting from the inside."

Willem sighed but didn't argue. Instead, he shifted his

pack and muttered, "Well, I suppose you're stubborn enough to make it."

François smiled faintly. "Then come. Let's see if this road is kinder than the one we left behind."

The three resumed their walk, their steps heavy with loss but steadier for the company. François glanced at Willem and Matthias. The horizon stretched before them, wide and open. They moved forward, not knowing where the road would lead but no longer facing it alone.

Only the Song Remains

The tavern stilled, the final note resonating like a ghost before decaying into silence.

Joos van den Rijm let the silence stretch, watching his audience through the dim glow of tallow candles. Some leaned forward as if the ghosts of François and Willem lingered in the air. Others avoided his gaze, lost in their thoughts.

At the far end of the tavern, the magistrate—who had scowled through most of the performance—gave a short, dry laugh. "A fine tale, minstrel. But we both know no one escapes history so neatly."

Van den Rijm swirled his drink, considering. "Ah, but history is a fickle thing. Some names vanish, others linger in song. Tell me, good sir, which would you rather be?"

The magistrate scoffed. "And what became of them, then? Your François and Willem?"

Van den Rijm smiled faintly. "That depends."

He leaned in slightly, voice dipping just enough to pull the crowd closer.

"I could tell you they vanished into the hills, free men beneath the open sky. I could tell you they were caught before dawn, dragged back to Bruges, and silenced before another sunrise."

He lifted his cup, his eyes flickering with something unreadable.

"Or I could tell you that some stories are meant to

linger—half truth, half dream, waiting for those with ears to hear them."

The embers in the hearth popped, sending a brief flicker of light across the room. A younger man near the bar—perhaps a journeyman, not unlike those who once sat here long ago—tilted his head. "The Bear has seen many men pass through its doors," he murmured. "This place has a way of holding on to its dead," the journeyman murmured. "Some echoes refuse to fade."

Van den Rijm chuckled and drained the last of his ale.

"Perhaps, my friend. But some ghosts," he said, rising from his seat, "are lucky enough to walk away."

With that, he slung his lute over his shoulder and disappeared into the night, leaving only the echoes of his song—and the unanswered question—behind him.

Give light, and the darkness will disappear
of itself.

— *Erasmus* (*1466–1536*)

Acknowledgments

Every book is a journey, and *Scapegoat* is no exception. Along its winding roads, I am guided, challenged, and encouraged by those walking beside me—sometimes offering a lantern, sometimes a compass, sometimes simply reminding me I am not wandering alone.

Kristyn Kamps, you are the steady hand on the map, keeping me moving forward even when the road ahead is uncertain. Your patience, unwavering belief, and countless conversations stretched over months and miles made this book possible.

Herb Chamberlain, you remind me that a story's power lies in its truth—even when that truth is difficult to face. Your keen eye for emotional depth, reflections on Willem's quiet emergence, and insights on pacing and foreshadowing continue to sharpen this book in ways I could not have achieved alone.

Leslie Polgar, you are my detail-keeper, ensuring that Bruges is not merely a setting but a living, breathing world. Your deep historical knowledge lends this story depth and credibility.

Larry Nickol, you are my compass in navigating language. Your guidance preserves the integrity of every line, ensuring that contemporary speech rhythms never overshadow the historical voice of this narrative.

Mary LaFever, your reflections on fear, understanding, and the weight of an ending that might better serve as a beginning reshape how I see this story.

Dick LaFever, you find the missing puzzle piece and place it exactly where it belongs. Your suggestion to reposition the Erasmus quote strengthens the continuity of the Preface, subtly but powerfully guiding the reader into the world of this book.

Benjamin Obler, my editor, you are both architect and builder, shaping the raw materials of this manuscript into something stronger, something truer. Your patience, insights, and the creative space you cultivate at Synthetic Prophetic (syntheticprophetic.com) continue to be sources of inspiration and support.

And Doug Hunter, my husband—you are my North Star, guiding me forward. Your honesty keeps me grounded, your unwavering faith in me keeps me striving, and your support makes this journey possible. Your impact on this book cannot be overstated.

To each of you—fellow travelers and guiding lights—I offer my deepest gratitude. This book is as much yours as it is mine.

—Donald Proffit

About the Author

Donald Proffit has been short-listed for the 2024 William Saroyan International Writing Prize in nonfiction. He holds degrees from Westminster Choir College, Rutgers University, and Bank Street College of Education in partnership with Parsons School of Design. Donald has trained with performance artist Ping Chong and studied at the Martha Graham Center of Contemporary Dance. His accolades include a John F. Kennedy Center Fellowship, two New Jersey Governor's Awards in Arts Education, and the D. Bennet Mazur Award for Lifetime Achievement.

He's the author of *Hardship, Alaska: A Memoir* (Epicenter Press, 2023), and the novel *The Object of His Affection* (Synthetic Prophetic, 2024).